# DIANA HARKER

# PEPPERMINT ORCHID

# ALSO BY D.E. HARKER

<u>The Knot Garden</u>

'A parachute drop over marshes on a moonless night; the ghost of a nun in an ancient manor house; strange music heard in the village church at night, heralding enemy raids; a secret tunnel to the sea; a Nazi plot; a foreign spy planted in a Cheshire village; the unravelled truth about a seventeenth century love affair; lost treasure – and an equal exuberance of characters.'

*Times Literary Supplement*

<u>Roman Graffiti</u>

'Another challenging story for children – Bright youngsters will find the story is fun to read and it will stimulate their interest in history.'

*The Independent on Sunday*

'The third in this much praised adventure series. A real cliff-hanging thriller that cleverly combines adventure, history and education in the kind of literary package that ought to provide a trademark for anyone contemplating writing for children.'

*Welsh Arts Council Literary Supplement*

<u>Saxon Summer and The Knot Garden</u>

'Both are rattling good yarns.'

*Daily Post*

<u>House of Secrets</u>

'A deftly organised, fast moving story going back in time – showing how sombre life can be, both in the 21st century and in a Victorian family.'

*Gillian Avery*

<u>Three Men in a Minor</u>

'I heartily recommend this book to you written by D.E. Harker. It's the story of three men who go off up to Galloway for a holiday in an old Morris Minor and of their adventures in that lovely part of Scotland.

It's humorous and it's enthralling. Told in the first person by one of the three, it's one of those books that you don't want to put down.'

*Vintage Enthusiasts*

Matador
9 Priory Business Park
Wistow Road, Kibworth, Leice LE8 0RX
Tel: 0116 2792299
Email: books@troubador.co.uk
Web: www.troubador.co.uk/matador

ISBN 9781780882581

British Library Cataloguing in Publication Data.
A catalogue record for this book is available from the British Library.

Typeset in 11pt Stempel Garamond by Troubador Publishing Ltd, Leicester, UK

**Matador** is an imprint of Troubador Publishing Ltd

Printed and bound in the UK by TJ International, Padstow, Cornwall

*For my family*

*Cover design*
*–Ava Harker*

# PROLOGUE                1894

He balanced precariously on one of the top branches of the giant amazonian redwood tree and felt it sway.

*Is it really worth it?* he wondered.

He allowed himself to look down for a dizzying second.

Far below, almost obscured by thick vegetation, Earle could just make out the tiny figure of the leader of the expedition – and very faintly, above the sound of chattering monkeys and screeching parakeets, he heard the warning shout.

'Come back down, you fool, while you still can – come down!'

But the sight of his prize, almost within reach, strengthened his resolve.

A snake slithered along a side branch, the vibrant colour of its skin caught by a momentary shaft of sun seen through dense foliage. He crawled forward.

'I must reach it, I must – or no one will ever believe me.'

Out of a patch of moss and lichen, the pale orchid was growing: perfect, beautiful and rare – the fragile rainbow orchid. He stretched out towards it and gently pulled the whole clump towards him. Now he noticed a subtle smell of mint; it was a relative of the exotic tiger orchid, said to have magical properties.

The branch he was balancing on suddenly cracked.

\*\*\*

In the steamy heat of the Tropical House at the zoo, there was a small sign in front of one of the orchids – a particularly beautiful one with large soft petals, the veins inside ran down in decreasing circles like a spiral:-

## RAINBOW ORCHID

*This rare species – a relative of the tiger orchid oncidium – was discovered on the 1894 expedition to the remote amazonian Chrystall Islands by the botanist Sir Howard Earle. It is believed to have magical properties.*

# ONE

There was hardly a sound to be heard, apart from the continuous muffled drone of the traffic three streets away. The house was silent as always. Alice gazed moodily out of the long sash window at the beige stucco house opposite. A damp November mist hung over everything – the bare trees, iron railings and the grey pavements. A thin cat sat motionless on an empty window box.

The air felt oppressive and strangely still, not just quiet but different, like the calm before a thunderstorm.

*I wish there'd be a huge storm – with great streaks of lightning and crashes of thunder – so loud that they'd rock the house... And change everything for ever,* she thought. *Some hope!*

Her spirits drooped and she turned back to her room. Inside was not much better – everything here was beige and grey too, relieved now and again by a little white. Her mother, who liked Alice to call her "Bunny" ('we really seem more like sisters,' she always said to her friends) had chosen the colour scheme for the house with her usual thoroughness. Pale beige walls throughout, grey spikey furniture, a darker grey for the carpets and white lampshades of strange design. Some of the curtains had been specially dyed to an exact neutral colour, although Alice just had a plain white roller blind in her bedroom.

'Of course, you have such amazing good taste, Bunny,' her friends said, as they perched uncomfortably on the stiff grey chairs at one of the Saturday night "at homes" the Frasers held regularly. 'Amazing good taste.'

Alice's father, or "Terry" as everyone, including Alice, called him, had once made a standard lamp out of a long and twisted piece of metal he had found in a salvage depot. It was much admired. 'You're so creative,' everyone said. Alice thought it was hideous.

She went to look at herself in the mirror. *I match the house,* she thought crossly: *grey cardigan and skirt, white shirt, pale skin and beige coloured hair.* She had a sudden longing for bright red hair, orange trousers, green sweater, rows of pink beads, yellow shoes, loud music, excitement – young friends of her own age.

She glanced at the geography homework spread out all over the white table – the questions on chief exports of Venezuela and the population and climate of Peru were unanswered.

'When you've finished your geography you and Connie can have a nice little expedition to the zoo,' Bunny had said brightly over the avocados at lunch.

Sundays always followed the same pattern. Flute practice for Alice in the morning for an hour, while

Bunny and Terry recovered from their "frantic" week by having an extra hour or two of sleep in their "off white" bedroom; then "project" time when Alice would pursue a fulfilling hobby, like oil painting, clay modelling or origami with much spreading round of newspaper to keep everything clean. Terry would look in for ten minutes and give some serious criticism. Then before lunch, she would clean out the hutch of her angora rabbit, Alabaster, which had been christened by her mother. She was fond of Alabaster but she had really wanted a parrot or a monkey.

Lunch, homework, then a little expedition or a walk or a visit to an exhibition while her parents worked on drawings and plans in the cold white studio at the top of the house.

A cup of herbal tea – part of Bunny's latest diet – and an intelligent read of the Sunday papers, with a chat on current affairs while, in winter, the fake, flickering flames of the gas "log" fire might be lit. This would be followed by bath, hair wash, supper and a little judicious look at a television programme and then bed. "Quality Hour" was just for Monday, Wednesday and Friday.

It was like a school curriculum; every minute accounted for and sometimes Alice felt she was in a prison – comfortable, clean, hygienic, and in perfect good taste but a prison none the less. If only she had a brother or a sister, or some cousins, or children who lived next door but there was no one to share things with. Her friend at school, Lucy Braithwaite, lived miles away and out of school hours she only saw her occasionally. Lucy played the harp and the viola so, with her parents approval, Alice sometimes had tea at Lucy's home after school, and now and again Lucy was dropped off at eleven Rosetti Grove to spend Saturday afternoon with Alice. She really enjoyed these rare treats. *If only I had a mobile,* she thought for the hundredth time, but her parents disapproved of them.

'Alice!' Connie's sharp voice sounded from below. 'Have you finished your homework?' Alice would rather have wrestled with the problems of the Peruvian climate than go to the zoo with Connie but she sighed and went to get her coat. She remembered that once, long ago, she had said 'No' to some suggestion her father had made for an outing to an art museum. She seemed to remember that she had even stamped her foot. Terry had said, with a cross smile, that she ought to be ashamed of herself when Bunny always went to such trouble to organise everything for her. She had been made to feel guilty. It had all been a long time ago.

'Come along – it'll be dark in a couple of hours, dear.' Connie's voice had mellowed for the benefit of Bunny, whose footsteps could be heard on the polished wax stairs coming down from the studio.

Pauline Constance was the latest (and most hated by Alice) in a long line of au pairs and housekeepers or "treasures" as Bunny called them. Of indeterminate age and colouring, her cold greyish eyes were hard as pebbles and belied the constant smile she wore. This smile deceived everyone, including Bunny who had blessed the day that Mrs Constance had appeared in answer to an advertisement for an "extra pair of hands required by overworked professional couple and eleven year old Alice".

No one was quite sure where she'd come from and it was too late to ask now. There'd once been some vague mention of a brother, Eric, and Alice had once glimpsed a framed photograph of a rather fierce looking young man through the open door of Connie's bedroom.

'Call me Connie,' she'd said immediately with her cold smile. 'I could start right away if you like.' And Bunny, desperate, with an overload of work, had agreed to both suggestions with relief. With Connie at the helm to deal with domestic details, she and Terry could devote their time to the architectural practice, apart from supervising Alice's intellectual activities.

As Alice put on her warm, camel-coloured school coat, she wondered if her school, Huxley House, had been chosen by her parents for the colour of the uniform.

'Cream and Camel,' Bunny had announced with satisfaction, 'and educationally very sound.' Although Alice had once overheard the pupils described as "forced rhubarb" – thin, pale and trying too hard and she felt it was true. The amount of homework was horrific, class places were pinned up daily and exam results were all important. Most girls went round with a perpetually tense and worried expression.

'That's right,' Bunny said brightly, all brisk efficiency in a pale smock, her light brown hair neat in a severe bob. 'Now don't forget to look out for the latest addition to the marsupial family.' She believed in never using short words where long ones would do.

'Come on, I'm nearly thirteen… I'm a bit old for staring at baby kangaroos,' Alice protested.

A frown flickered over Bunny's face. 'Take your

sketch pad and crayons then and we'll give a critical appraisal of your efforts when you return.'

'Oh, a baby kangaroo, how lovely, that will be nice,' Connie gushed sentimentally. She had gushed like that when she had first seen Alabaster but had not been near him since.

After the carefully regulated temperature inside number eleven, the air outside struck cold and damp. 'Sooner we get there, sooner we'll be back,' Connie said grimly, striding out at a quick pace.

It was a long, boring walk to the zoo… streets, houses, churches, traffic and now and then a square with a few bare trees fenced in by iron railings; Alice knew it by heart. She trudged behind. A boring evening stretched ahead – a cup of blackcurrant tea, she'd have to finish her geography and maths homework, some Shakespeare she had to learn, a look at the financial and current affairs page in the newspapers, bath, a plate of wheaty puffs and a thought provoking documentary programme on television. She was always hungry and thought sometimes that Connie was starving her.

'What are you hanging back for – for goodness sake hurry up!' They crossed a busy road and Connie strode off into a quieter street.

*What would I rather be doing?* Alice thought to herself, as she often did. *I'd rather be cooking potatoes in a roaring bonfire at the end of a large, untidy garden and wearing a filthy pair of dungarees together with lots of friends, followed by grilled sausages and hide and seek. Or a party somewhere sunny and warm with loud music and lots of cream cakes, green jelly and Coca Cola. Or,* more realistically, she'd rather be sitting in front of Lucy's real coal fire, toasting crumpets and reading her comics or her sister's magazines, and making secret plans for the time when they'd both be hairdressers on a cruise ship.

Alice had had a nasty shock recently when Lucy had said, 'I'm leaving Huxley House at the end of term. I'm going to Parkwood High. Mum said it's not so pressurised or pressured or something.'

'Oh no!' Alice felt her stomach sink with dismay. She found school a struggle – Lucy was the only good thing about it and she wished she could leave too and go to Parkwood High; she'd been passed it and seen the modern buildings and groups of relaxed looking boys and girls coming out of the gates. There would also be no Zelda Hulton-Price there. At the thought of Zelda her stomach sank even further and she felt quite sick with worry.

They had nearly reached the zoo and it was starting to rain now; a soft drizzle which prompted Connie to stop and put up her small umbrella. *Was that a distant rumble of thunder?*

'As soon as we get there, I'm going for a pot of tea. You can wander round the animals if you like.' She quickened her step again, grudgingly letting Alice share some of the shelter of the umbrella.

There were not many people at the zoo – a few family groups in anoraks and macs laughing together at the antics of the penguins and the chimpanzees, and some children had gathered round the sea lions' pool to wait for feeding time. It was feeding time now as far as Connie was concerned, and she went off to find a table in the restaurant away from any draughts, after arranging to meet Alice at the Tropical House at four o'clock.

A keeper appeared with two buckets and made his way over to the sea-lion enclosure, where a little murmur of excitement went up from the small groups huddled together. Alice put her hand out to see if it had stopped raining but she couldn't really tell, the air was so damp. She drew her small sketch pad and pencil out of her pocket with cold clammy hands and looked around for inspiration. One of the sea lions was posed on the top of a rock, clapping his flippers and hooting loudly. The noise reminded her of her parents "at home" evening last night – it sounded just like Annabel Prescott's laugh. She and her husband, James Prescott (of Prescott's Pile Drivers) were great friends of Bunny and Terry, and Alice had been summoned to play her flute for the assembly.

'Bravo!' Annabel had shouted at the end of Mozart, clapping loudly, although she had talked all the way through it. 'Wasn't that brilliant? How old are you now – ten?'

'Nearly thirteen,' Alice had muttered.
Annabel had given one of her laughs – 'What are they feeding you on, bird seed?'
Alice looked at the sea lions catching their fish. 'What are they feeding you on, bird seed?' she said aloud in a good imitation of Annabel's affected voice.

She jabbed her pencil on to the paper and tried to draw the keeper with a fish flying through the air. Terry would have dashed off a witty sketch with a few deft pencil lines in a couple of minutes but Alice's effort looked stiff and childish. She could hear Bunny trying to defend the picture to Terry. 'It has a certain naïve charm, don't you think?' she would say, trying to hide her disappointment.

'Wot's that there – a monkey tossing a pancake?' A young boy, one of a lively family party – cheerful and chattering – had come over to see what Alice was working on. She put her hand over the page and coloured slightly.

A girl of about her own age pulled him away. 'You can talk! You can't even tell one end of a pencil from another.' She grinned at Alice, showing lovely, even white teeth. She was very pretty and wore a large floppy red bow in her black curls. Someone called her.

'Come on, Amy. We're going to see the parrots when we've got our ice-creams,' and they gave an imitation of a loud parrot whistle.

Alice gave her slight, tight little smile at the other girl, then watched her being drawn back into the centre of the noisy happy group. *Lucky her*, she thought. *Lucky, lucky her – to be part of it*. She didn't think she could be noisy if she tried, she wouldn't know how to shout and laugh like that.

She tried to concentrate on her sketch again but kept looking at the retreating figures: the one they called Amy, the cheeky one who'd looked at her drawing, an older teenage girl; a young man who was carrying a child of two or three who was wriggling and protesting, and two other children throwing a crumpled paper bag to each other, pushing and jostling, dodging and jumping and all the time keeping up a lively commentary as if they were playing in a basket-ball match and they were the Harlem Globe Trotters.

Amy glanced back once over her shoulder at Alice and then they were all gone, round the corner in the direction of the Tropical House and it was suddenly quiet again. Even the sea lions were subdued now after their meal. The keeper had vanished and the few spectators had dispersed.

Alice put her sketch book back in her pocket and looked at her watch. It was half past three. Should it be the giraffes next or her favourites, the polar bears?

For some reason there was only one bear in the compound today. Polo stood high and mighty on the largest rock, gazing into the distance in sad isolation. It started to rain more heavily but he didn't budge. Alice sympathised with him.

A few people nearby started to dash for shelter to the restaurant. Not wishing to spend more time with Connie than she need, Alice ran in the opposite direction – to the Tropical House, where palm trees and parrots lived in an equatorial heat.

The hot air met her in a rush as she pushed open the door and she felt as if her damp hair and coat were steaming. It was like stepping into another world. Bird calls echoed round the glass house and jungle greenery. A green parrot caught Alice's eye and she watched while it went through its tricks for her benefit; walking upside down on a thin branch and standing on one leg while scratching its head with the other, then ruffling his feathers and finishing with a loud cackle of laughter.

A special section of the Tropical House was devoted to palms and plants; banana trees and great trailing tendrils of oriental honeysuckle covered the glass, while brilliantly coloured flowers of unknown species bloomed in wild profusion.

In the centre, in a wide stone circular well, were the orchids, exotic and delicate and in the centre was one so unusual that Alice leant forward to read its name. "RAINBOW ORCHID" from the Chrystall Islands believed to have magical properties.' *Magical properties, I wonder what...* Alice's thoughts were interrupted by more squawks and shrieks, not from the birds this time but human ones. The group she had seen by the sea lions was approaching from the opposite side of the orchids and through the leaves Alice could see them joking, laughing and arguing while the youngest was, this time, crying to be picked up. They were completely absorbed in each other.

'Stop fooling around with that paper bag can't you!' The older girl grabbed one of the younger children and shook him gently. 'This is meant to be your birthday treat, isn't it? Look at all these lovely flowers.' But he wasn't interested.

'I wanted to go and watch Spurs.'

'Here – throw it to me,' one of the others shouted and the bag was up in the air again.

There was a sudden flash of lightning.

Alice saw Amy's face through the foliage – she was looking at the others, then, turning back to the blossom, caught Alice's eye. The two smiled at each other. Reaching forward to smell the pale, almost translucent petals of the flower, Alice thought yearningly that it would be wonderful to belong to a large, noisy, friendly family like that.

*Oh, I wish...*

# TWO

It had been an even noisier morning than usual that Sunday at number six Disraeli Drive. Danny was celebrating his ninth birthday and had been awake since six o'clock that morning.

He'd taken his pillow and banged it over the heads of his brothers – Aldous, eight and Jimmy, three – who slept in bunk beds in the same room. Dad had banged on the wall which had woken Evalina and Amy. The dog they were looking after for some friends started to bark and no one could get back to sleep after that, so everyone, except Uncle Edgar, who was staying in the caravan in the back garden, got up and had breakfast and Danny opened his presents.

Amy cleared away and washed the dishes, helped unwillingly by Aldous who wanted to go to the park with Danny and his new football. It was no good asking Evalina to help – she'd just painted her fingernails, and Dad was listening to something on the radio while

Jimmy kept twiddling the knobs and turning it up too loud.

'All right, you two,' Dad said to Danny and Aldous, 'we'll go and try out that new football and we'll all go and see Mum before lunch – visiting hours are easier on Sundays.'

'I want to come too,' Jimmy cried.

'I said we'll *all* go, didn't I?' Dad said patiently.

'I want to play *football*.' Jimmy didn't like to be left out of anything.

'No. You're staying with Amy to help her make a special cake. You can have the scrapings, lucky thing,' Aldous said firmly, but Jimmy couldn't be bribed so easily. 'I can have those *after*,' he said after thinking about it.

Amy had forgotten that she'd promised to make a cake. The trouble was, with Mum in hospital having her varicose veins dealt with, she seemed to have so much more to do – everyone relied on her for clean clothes, food, feeding the animals and the shopping. Evalina was hopeless, always in a dream; if anything was left to her it never got done. Dad helped when he could with some of the shopping, but he had so much travelling in his job at the Met Office weather bureau each day and then his work as "unofficial vet" to the neighbourhood, that in his free moments he collapsed into the nearest armchair. Danny was accident prone – always dropping things or somehow breaking them and he'd nearly set the house on fire the day he'd tried to iron one of Dad's shirts.

Aldous was slightly better but would generally

manage to be missing just when he was most needed, and Uncle Edgar... well it was useless to expect him to do anything practical. He was said, in the family, to be the artistic one and "must have his chance" as Mum always said. He was twenty-five, and her youngest brother and she still seemed to treat him as if he were the same age as Jimmy. Even when he'd given up a perfectly good job at the Gas Board to let his "music ride over him and catch the right beat", as he put it, Mum had given her support :'He must have his chance.'

'Yeah – we'll see what happens,' Uncle Edgar had said easily, smiling his big lazy smile.

'I'll tell you what'll happen – nothing!' Dad had replied sarcastically. He hated the noises that came from the caravan in the garden at all times of the day and night, preferring traditional jazz himself. He and Uncle Edgar had loud, noisy rows.

*Thomas is the lucky one*, Amy thought, as she beat up some margarine and sugar and gave Jimmy the job of greasing two baking tins, *lucky to be at college in a room of his own with peace and quiet to study his accountancy*. He was going to be the financial wizard of the family; she was going to be the doctor. She cracked some eggs into a bowl; she hadn't fed the rabbits or the cats yet. When would she get a moment to do her prep? And there was the project on Florence Nightingale to start.

The front door bell rang and Jimmy knocked over the bag of flour as he struggled to get down from the chair he was standing on. He ran to look through the letter box to see who it was.

'It's only me!' The loud voice and laugh of Auntie

Seely reached Amy as she stood looking furiously at the spilt flour.

'Come on now, leave that mess. I'll give you a hand with it later.' Auntie Seely sat down heavily on Jimmy's chair and put the skate board she'd brought for Danny on the table. She'd also brought her daughter, Chrissie with her and her poodle who'd got something in his paw.

'Dad will have a look at it,' Amy said, 'Would you like some coffee?' Although she hoped the answer would be no, she knew Auntie Seely lived for her cups of coffee.

'I thought you'd never ask,' she laughed.

'All of us are meeting round at Kev's house this afternoon – you coming?' Chrissie asked. She was Amy's age and they both went to King's Wood School.

'Sorry – just too much to do.' Amy filled the kettle while Chrissie examined Danny's birthday cards.

'Like what?' she said without looking round.

'Got to make a cake, fix some lunch, visit Mum and I've got a great pile of prep to do – biology… And…' Amy put spoonfuls of instant coffee into some mugs while keeping half an eye on Jimmy who was prodding the poodle.

Chrissie studied a large, brightly coloured card of some footballers. 'Everyone says you're getting stuck up – you never go anywhere these days.'

'It's not that, you know it isn't,' Amy said angrily. She jerked Jimmy away from the poodle who was now snarling, then banged the mugs of coffee down on the table.

'I'm only saying what everyone says.' Chrissie said.

'You want to get out more – enjoy yourself. What do

they say – all work and no play...' and Aunt Seely put her feet up on the kitchen stool and took a mouthful of coffee, which burnt her tongue.

'More milk, quickly – why did you make it so hot!'

'Perhaps when Mum's back, it'll be a bit easier and then...'

But Aunt Seely cut in with a laugh 'Oh, she'll have to rest up for weeks, take it from me – legs up, like this and no lifting heavy things. I remember when...' and she went off into the very familiar story of her own operation, adding one or two some friends had undergone for good measure.

Amy had cleaned up the flour, popped the chocolate cake into the oven and had finished peeling the vegetables for lunch by the time Aunt Seely and Chrissie decided it was time to go home.

'That cake smells good.' Aunt Seely sniffed the air appreciatively. 'Tell your mum to make the most of her holiday, I'll get along to see her if I can – no promises – great heavens, what's that?' A loud, high-pitched noise reached their ears.

'Just Uncle Edgar trying out a new theme,' Amy explained. A quick rhythm on the drum was followed by a fierce rattling of a tambourine. 'He's trying to write the music down.'

Aunt Seely said sadly, 'That Edgar... what's going to become of him... Waste of time,' she shook her head.

'Must have his chance,' Amy found herself repeating her mother's words.

'What'll I tell Kev then?' Chrissie asked, winding a long yellow scarf around her neck.

'Tell him whatever you like!' Amy banged the door after them.

The telephone rang and Evalina appeared for a moment at the top of the stairs to see if it was one of her boyfriends. 'It's Thomas,' Amy shouted up, 'ringing up to see how Mum is.'

But after satisfying himself that the operation had gone well, his voice became more urgent – 'Amy, who's there with you?'

'Jimmy's here and Dad and the others will be back in a minute – Evalina's upstairs – who d'you want to speak to?'

'You! Listen, I'm in big trouble,' his voice seemed to fade.

'Thomas – are you there? What's happened – tell me.'

'Mustn't tell anyone – especially not Mum – don't want her worried. It's… oh no. Someone's coming…' There was silence for a moment.

'Thomas!' Amy shouted.

'Keep cool,' but his voice didn't sound reassuring. 'There is someone coming – can't explain now – I'll try again later…' He put the phone down to Amy's worry and frustration.

There was no way of ringing Thomas back as she knew there was just a public telephone in his hall of residence at college – the line was always busily engaged if they tried and his mobile was always dead.

The poodle and the dog they were minding for friends were snarling at each other as Amy took the cake out of the oven to cool. What was the trouble that Thomas was in? He hadn't given any clue and she wasn't able to tell anyone.

Her aunt's poodle started barking frenziedly at a long, slim figure which had loomed up out of the grey mist outside the glass window of the kitchen door. Uncle Edgar was coming to see if there were any signs of Sunday lunch which he shared with the family. He was snapping his fingers and nodding his head in time to a rhythm which only he could hear. His eye alighted on the mixing bowl with the remains of the cake mixture.

'What's cooking?' He ran an expert finger round the bowl and popped some into his mouth.

Jimmy, who had been experimenting with the "loud" knob on the radio again, caught sight of his promised cake scrapings disappearing into Edgar's mouth and started howling. The vegetables, put on earlier, boiled over and Dad, Aldous and Danny arrived back from the park. Amy had to push the worry about Thomas to the back of her mind.

\*\*\*

After lunch when they arrived at the hospital, Mum was sitting up in bed in a pale blue, knitted bed jacket. She put her arms out to hug her family and give Danny a big birthday kiss.

'Yes – everything's fine' they all reassured her, keeping their private worries to themselves. They all seemed to speak at once then suddenly there was nothing left to say. Mum took some money out of her purse and handed it to Danny. 'Here – birthday treat for you all to go to the zoo this afternoon.'

Amy saw some of the other patients nodding and

smiling at them. She clung to Mum when they said goodbye. 'I'll be home soon.' Mum gave her a special squeeze. Jimmy cried – he missed her!

They took a bus to the zoo: Dad had said that it would probably rain, 'And there may be an unseasonal thunderstorm,' he warned. He had to attend to a neighbour's cat and Auntie Seely's poodle, but a boyfriend of Evalina's joined them and he was quite a help with Jimmy. Amy wondered if he was going to stay for tea and if the chocolate cake would go round. She thought of her prep sitting on top of the small table in the room she shared with her sister; even if she'd stayed behind this afternoon there would have been no chance to work quietly. Uncle Edgar always watched television on a Sunday – football or an old film – and usually some of his friends came round, talking and laughing in the room just underneath Amy's. Their next door neighbour usually spent Sunday afternoon tuning up his motorbike. There never seemed to be any peace and quiet anywhere, ever.

Dad had given her some money for a fish and chip supper that evening, so she wouldn't have to think about what to eat, that was a relief. It was starting to rain slightly; Dad had been right as usual. Amy looked out of the bus window at the grey, damp afternoon and realised they were almost there. Evalina and her friend, Paul, were deep in conversation. Their heads close together in a world of their own.

'Come on, we're there!' Amy shouted and gathered everyone together, just managing to restrain Jimmy from jumping off the bus while it was still going, which he was always trying to do.

'Let's go to the lions first,' Aldous said when they'd paid their entrance money.

'I want to see the monkeys!' Jimmy danced up and down.

'Look – whose birthday is it?' Danny demanded, 'I can choose whatever I want and I choose...' He closed his large brown eyes for a moment while he considered, 'I choose the reptile house!'

'I'm not going near any snakes – you know I can't stand them,' Evalina shuddered and Paul put a protective arm around her. 'We'll go this way to the sea lions.' And she turned smartly on her black high heels while the others followed. They knew what her temper was like if she was crossed and roused from her normal preoccupied air, and they also knew her habit of digging those sharp scarlet nails into the fleshy part of their arms if she grabbed them suddenly.

They stood watching the sea lions being fed. 'Evalina looks like a seal,' Aldous nudged Danny, and Amy, overhearing, laughed with them and agreed. In her sleek, shiny black mac glistening with spots of rain, black tights and shoes, her elbows stretched out as she yawned with boredom, Evalina did look seal-like.

Jimmy was crying to be picked up again and Amy turned round to him. As she did so, she noticed further along the wall of the enclosure, the pale, still figure of a girl about the same age as her. She was concentrating intently on something she was working on – a sketch perhaps – and around her, Amy seemed to sense an aura of peace and serenity, of stillness and calm: she seemed to be on her own.

They drew nearer to her, Danny and Aldous fighting now and Jimmy was still whingeing to be picked up. 'We'll go and get an ice-cream,' Evalina bribed him. 'Point me in the direction of the nearest kiosk!'

'This way!' Danny pointed to a sign and ran ahead. He peeped over the arm of the girl who was drawing something and tried to guess what it was, 'Wot's that then – a monkey tossing a pancake?' He shrugged his shoulders as the girl flushed and put her hand over the page.

Amy felt embarrassed by his rudeness and intrusion into the girl's privacy and pulled him away roughly. 'You can talk – you can't even tell one end of a pencil from another!' She grinned apologetically. The rest of the family had overtaken her. Paul had swung Jimmy up into the air and was carrying him now.

'Come on Amy, we're going to see the parrots when we've got our ice-creams!' Aldous yelled and gave a loud imitation of a parrots' whistle.

The girl gave a small, shy smile at Amy and watched as the others went off to get their ices; Amy glanced back once over her shoulder and then they turned the corner and found the kiosk. There was a noisy discussion while they all decided what to have. Amy preferred a bar of chocolate – she felt cold enough without freezing herself more with an iced lolly or ice cream. She wondered if Thomas would ring back that evening and how she would be able to speak to him without everyone else joining in? Was he ill? It was raining more heavily now. Amy's red bow on her hair was soaking wet and dripping down her neck. The Tropical House was a warm sanctuary.

Jimmy found a green parrot who had a surprising vocabulary of swear words and was quite happy to stay there shouting to him while the parrot kept a beady orange eye on Danny and Aldous, who were now kicking the paper bag to each other using two potted plants as a goal post.

'Come on, that's enough of that,' Paul grasped a protesting Jimmy by the hand, 'we're off to the aquarium.'

'Not likely,' Evalina said firmly, 'my feet are killing me. Lead me to a cup of tea.'

'To soak your feet in?' Danny asked, giving the paper bag a vicious kick.

Amy wandered ahead in amongst large ferns and palm trees. Strange and rare flowers blossomed in the heat. Evalina paused to admire a giant bright, yellow lily. 'I'd love a pair of earrings that shade…' The paper bag caught her smartly on the side of the neck. 'Stop fooling around with that paper bag can't you?' Evalina shook Danny by the shoulders and then remembered it was his birthday, while Amy wandered over to look at the display of orchids in the centre of the Tropical House. One special orchid in the middle caught her eye, with large soft petals entwined with pale green foliage. She reached out a hand wanting to touch the fragile silken bloom and through the leaves, standing on the other side of the plant, came face to face with the pale, calm girl she had seen before – still alone. Lit up by a sudden flash of lightning, they smiled at each other. Behind her, Amy could hear her family, joking shouting, and arguing.

She leant forward to see if the flower had a smell that matched its beauty. *How wonderful,* she thought, *how wonderful to be like that other girl, so quiet and still, to have a bit of peace and time to myself and to be on my own for once. I wish...*

# THREE

The smell from the orchid was unexpectedly powerful and an unusual one for a flower: peppermint... Alice sniffed deeply. The veins on the inside of the petals ran in decreasing circles like a spiral with no end; the scent seemed to pass right through her whole body and she had the strange feeling of floating above herself for what seemed like minutes. Thoughts spun round in her head and she could see pictures of her life – the school she disliked, her mother's opinionated friends with their loud voices, her lonely room, the cold and mean "Connie", Zelda Hulton-Price – then suddenly she was down to earth again.

She seemed to be gazing at the orchid from another viewpoint and, looking round, found she was surrounded by the family she had been watching, but the girl they called Amy had gone. They were all smiling except for the youngest who, for some reason, tugged at her skirt and asked to be carried. Without knowing exactly why, she smiled at him, bent down and picked him up, and it seemed the most natural thing in the world. Then they were all moving towards a door at the side. The older girl was prodding her in the back. 'Cup of tea,' she muttered and Alice found herself propelled forward with the others pushing and jostling around her. 'But I...' she started to say but no one took the slightest notice. She knew it was time to meet Connie but felt reluctant to break away from the group.

It was pouring now and struggling through the rain, holding the child who seemed to get heavier every moment, Alice bumped into someone coming out of the tea shop with a red umbrella.

'Oh, I'm sorry...' she began and then saw that it was Connie.

But instead of dragging her off and being cross, Connie just muttered, 'Why can't you look where you're going,' and walked purposefully away in the direction of the Tropical House. It was as if they'd never met, she'd shown no sign of recognition; looking at Alice but without seeing her. Should she run after her? She felt shocked at being ignored like that but before she could decide what to do, the others had made a quick decision to abandon the idea of tea and catch a bus home. The young man quickly lifted the child out of Alice's arms, the two young boys each took one of her hands and with the older girl pushing from behind they all ran out into the rain, towards the zoo exit and then to the bus stop where a bus was just approaching.

They were all gasping for breath as they sank into seats upstairs.

'My feet, my feet,' moaned the older girl kicking off her high heels. 'Who's got the fish and chip money?'

Alice sat by the window. How had she come to be sitting here in this bus heading off in the wrong direction with a family she didn't know but who seemed calmly to accept her as one of themselves? She felt frightened as it was getting dark now but she also felt excited, as if what she was doing was perfectly normal and right.

'Come on Amy, hand it over,' one of the boys was shouting, 'Dad gave you the money at the hospital – I saw him.'

'Amy!' The long red fingernails of the other girl poked Alice in the back, 'What's the matter with you? Come on, snap out of it.' She clicked her fingers and Alice turned round startled. Why were they calling her Amy?

'The money – the money, in your pocket!' The boys shouted. Automatically, Alice put her hand in her pocket, which felt larger than usual, and drew out a bright green purse which she didn't recognise. The others seized it. Alice was still looking at her hand which held the purse. It wasn't her own pale hand with thin fingers and the small scar left by a fall on the gravel she'd had when she was six; it was brown and capable looking with longer nails and a bracelet of pink coral beads round the wrist. She couldn't speak. She looked at her other hand and then at her reflection in the window of the bus. Looking back at her was the face of Amy; pretty, lively, the red bow now drooping damply on the black curls. She put up her hand to feel her hair, thick and springy. Now she looked down at them, the clothes were Amy's too.

'Why so blue? Cheer up! It may never happen!' The young man with the child still on his lap tapped her on the shoulder.

Alice tried a smile and looked at her reflection again. White even teeth, a dimple at the side of her mouth. The family thought she was Amy. She remembered wishing desperately to belong to a family like this and somehow, miraculously, she had got her wish. It had happened! Perhaps if she pinched herself she'd wake up and find it was all a dream but she realised she didn't want to – not yet. She sank back in her seat and relaxed, smiling again – no wonder Connie hadn't recognised her. She'd telephone home later – they'd all be worried and looking for her – but just for a little while she'd make the most of it and enjoy herself.

The bus was gathering speed, lurching from side to side along roads unfamiliar to Alice, past blocks of flats and shops she'd never seen before and lit up by street lamps; areas of park land, small factories and rows of houses where she could glimpse families watching television or having tea. 'Come on!' Her family were edging towards the stairs and Alice followed, wondering where she was.

'Paul and I'll go to the chippy, you take the others home and put the kettle on.' Alice found herself standing in the wet street with the three boys.

'With vinegar for me, Evalina,' one of the boys shouted after the other two, who went off hand-in-hand, in the direction of a row of brightly lit shops.

Which way was home? She was meant to lead the way but had no idea where they were going. She stood still. 'You go ahead – we'll come on more slowly – he's a bit tired,' she looked down at the little child.

'We'll look after Jimmy – you go on ahead and do the table – you said you'd got some crackers. Have you done my cake?'

Alice didn't know what he was talking about 'Perhaps,' she said in her new voice, slightly lower in tone and louder than usual, 'and perhaps not,' she added, taking Jimmy firmly by the hand. 'Go on now,' and to her surprise the boys accepted her authority and led the way down a road to the right.

'Want lots of icing on the cake,' Jimmy looked up at her, 'lots of icing.'

The two boys were going too fast and Alice became frightened she might lose sight of them. 'Hey!' she called.

'Danny!' Jimmy shouted joining in.

'Danny!' Alice yelled loudly and the older one of the two turned round. 'Wait for us – Jimmy wants to keep up with you!'

Two more turns to the left and they were in a tree lined road of detached and semi-detached houses. Disraeli Drive, Alice read.

At the gate marked number six, they turned in. The lights were on in the sitting room and before the front door was opened, various noises could be heard coming from inside. The whole house seemed to throb and vibrate with the sound of dogs barking, loud music with a persistent underlying beat and the sound of laughter and talk.

Alice stood back, afraid to go in. She was expected to

be one of the family and it would be taken for granted that she knew everyone and all about them and she knew nothing. Perhaps she should run away – but where? The door opened and a very tall man in a bright flowered shirt stood there, blocking the light from the hall.

'Where's that birthday boy, then? We've composed a tune specially for you. Come on in out of the cold.'

Evalina and Paul had caught up with them. 'What took you so long? I'd have thought you'd have had everything ready by now,' Evalina said crossly to Alice.

They all piled into the hall and Alice immediately felt surrounded by warmth and colour, brightly patterned carpet and yellow walls, and pictures of far away, sun-drenched places.

In the sitting room, the television was on and round it sat a couple of young men who were strumming guitars or beating a rhythm on a small drum. Alice went to warm her hands at the coal fire roaring away in the grate.

'My cake.' Danny tugged at her arm. *He must be the birthday boy and wants his birthday cake*, Alice thought. The doorbell rang.

'It's Aunt Seely come for her dog. Where's Dad?'

Dad emerged from another room holding a struggling poodle. He glared at the three round the television set. 'Out! I've warned you, Edgar, if you want to make that noise you call music, you can do it in your caravan!' he said to the one wearing the flowered shirt. The doorbell rang again.

'Aldous – go and let your aunt in!' A large plump woman heaved herself into the room, shaking her head when she saw Edgar and his companions.

'Come to me, my baby.' She held out her hands to the poodle while Dad explained briefly about its paw.

'Thanks for the skateboard, Aunt Seely,' Danny said, 'just what I wanted.'

'Happy birthday, Danny. How was your poor mother?' She bent down and gave him a big kiss. 'She's going to have to take things easy for a long time.' (*Where was "mother"?* Alice wondered) 'I hope I'm going to taste some of that cake I saw Amy making this morning,' She went on.

*Well, at least the cake is made,* Alice thought with relief.

'Yeah – when are we going to eat – I'm starving,' Aldous complained and everyone looked at Alice. Her anorak had started to steam from standing too close to the fire.

'Amy's on fire!' Jimmy cried.

Alice murmured something about taking off her coat and left the room. She was obviously expected to produce a birthday tea.

Leaving her anorak in the hall, she peered into the room behind the sitting room. It was a large kitchen – dining room. Warm and colourful, a lived-in homely room with children's' paintings stuck on the wall, a pair of budgies in a cage by the window, a dog asleep in a basket by the stove and in the middle, a large table covered by a blue and white gingham table cloth. A lovely room in complete contrast to the kitchen at Rosetti Grove – white and clinical and always cool.

On the work-top by the sink, Alice saw a chocolate cake ready to be iced. She'd never iced a cake before and she didn't think Bunny had either. They rarely had cakes at home.

Evalina popped her head round the door. 'I put the fish and chips in the oven to keep warm in case you're wondering where they are. Where's that tea – I'm spitting feathers!' And she vanished.

Alice filled the electric kettle and plugged it in.

*Icing, icing…* she opened the cupboards and found a packet of icing sugar. *Yes that must be a vital ingredient. Cocoa? Yes and I'll mix them together,* she thought, finding a bowl and a spoon. The result was powdery. She looked in the cupboard again. Mayonnaise, that might help and perhaps something called "chilli relish", which was a nice red colour. She tipped in a lot of that.

She mixed them all together and was pleased by the texture. "Texture" was a word frequently used by Bunny and Terry and she knew it was important.

The kettle was boiling and a huge rose-painted tea pot waited on the side. She didn't know how much Indian tea to put in so she just guessed, and then hurriedly slopped the icing in the middle of the chocolate sponge and spread it over the top. There was something lacking. Alice looked round the kitchen for inspiration and found it in a large potted plant with blue flowers. Tweaking off one of the blooms, she placed it in the centre of the cake and stood back to admire the effect; that looked much better – quite artistic. 'Quite art nouveau, my dear,' she said aloud, imitating one of Bunny's friends.

'What d'you say?' Dad put his head round the door this time. 'Oh, I like that,' he said looking at the cake. 'I put some crackers away from last Christmas. I'll just fetch them.'

A great number of blue mugs and plates were put on the table as well as cans of coke to supplement the tea, and suddenly the kitchen was crowded with people. The fish and chips were enjoyed, crackers were pulled and paper hats worn at odd angles.

'Shame Mum and Thomas aren't here with us,' Dad said.

'We'll have to take her a piece of my cake to the hospital,' Danny shouted, waving the bread knife ready to make the first cut.

*So, Mum's in hospital,* Alice thought, filing away the information in her mind, *but who's Thomas?*

Danny closed his eyes and plunged the knife deep into the cake, making a wish. Then everyone sang "Happy Birthday to you, squashed tomatoes and stew".

'Uncle Edgar's written some special song,' Aldous announced.

The very tall young man with the flowery shirt smiled broadly. 'When I've had my cake.'

Dad helped Danny cut the cake into lots of pieces and Aunt Seely reached for the biggest. She took a huge bite and closed her eyes: when she opened them, they started watering… Tears ran down her cheeks.

'Help, I've been poisoned!' she gasped.

'Water, water.' She pointed to her wide open mouth. 'I'm on fire!'

Trying to be helpful, Aldous fetched a large jug of water and threw it over her. There was a terrible silence, then Jimmy clapped his hands.

'Again!' he shouted. 'More!'

Aunt Seely exploded with fury. 'You *stupid* boy!' Mopping at her face with a hanky, she glared at Danny, who was shaking with laughter, and gathered up her yapping poodle.

'Aldous, apologise.' Dad was attempting to look stern.

'Mark my words... those boys...' but words failed Aunt Seely. Still coughing and spluttering she went, slamming the door loudly behind her.

Aldous said sullenly, 'Well, it was *her* fault, she said...'

Alice felt a momentary pang of guilt but no one blamed her and everyone was laughing now and sampling the cake, poking fingers into the icing and licking their fingers.

Hot, hot, hot was the general opinion: different and tasty in small amounts but not something they'd risk taking to Mum.

Uncle Edgar suddenly twanged his guitar and, with one of his friends providing the rhythm on the drum, sang his own composition "Streetwise". It seemed to have little to do with the birthday celebrations but no one seemed to mind.

Listening to the song, Alice suddenly realised she felt happy and content and even found herself swaying a little in time to the catchy tune. Suddenly it stopped. 'Sorry folks – can't seem to get the words right for the next bit, back to the drawing board, I guess.' Uncle Edgar grinned.

'Well, Paul and I are off,' Evalina said as the plates

were starting to be piled up. 'Friend's party,' she explained. 'Don't forget you promised to do that bit of ironing,' she said to Alice. Uncle Edgar and his friends also melted away as if by magic, leaving Dad, the boys and Alice to clean up.

'Aldous and I'll do the dishes,' Dad said to Alice. 'You go and get on with your homework. Must work hard if you're going to college like Thomas.'

*So that explained Thomas. Where was her homework?* she wondered. Upstairs probably. There were three bedrooms upstairs: Mum and Dad's with lots of family photos, one with bunk beds with posters of footballers, half-made models of aircraft and dirty socks all over the place, and the third must be the one she shared with Evalina. Jewellery, a cream satin blouse on a hanger and a red wig on a polystyrene stand caught Alice's eye. A frilly lampshade hung from the ceiling over two neat beds, under one of which were assorted high heeled shoes. The dressing table was cluttered with make-up and a small table in the corner was equally cluttered with books and papers, which had a familiar look: school work! She picked up an exercise book. It had a name on the front – AMY FORMICA.

In the sitting room below, Danny and Jimmy were having a row over a television programme. Uncle Edgar and friends were trying out a new theme which seemed to be coming from the back garden; the same bar repeated again and again, loud and insistent. It seemed to have woken up the dog downstairs who had started to bark.

Alice looked at the pile of books. She should really

go downstairs and telephone her parents – what could she say? She knew she'd have to think of something very soon.

Footsteps were banging up the stairs accompanied by sounds of someone crying. The door of the bedroom was pushed open and the tear-stained face of Jimmy peeped round. He shuffled in clutching an old blanket and sobbing. 'I want Mum. Want Mum.'

Alice went over to him and tried to comfort him by putting her arms round his shoulders awkwardly. He turned to her, clinging to her waist.

'Don't worry, Mum'll be home soon.' She hoped she sounded reassuring and hoped she was saying the right thing.

'Want her now,' and he started hammering at her legs with his hard little fists.

'Look – it must be your bedtime,' she said a bit stiffly. It must be her bedtime too, she thought, she was usually having a glass of milk in her pale beige bedroom at this time of night. Perhaps she could divert his attention. 'You go and get ready and then… I'll read you a story as a treat.'

He looked up briefly, his eyes swimming with tears, 'You always read to me.'

'Well, a special new story then,' Alice said desperately.

'No, want Frog.' He went into his room but couldn't find his pyjamas. Alice remembered Evalina's mention of some ironing – was there a stack of it piled up somewhere waiting for her? She opened a drawer and found a pair.

'Here you are,' and she went downstairs to get him a glass of milk.

The telephone rang. Dad left the jazz tape he was listening to in the kitchen and went to answer it. 'For you, Amy,' he called. He had to call twice before Alice realised, with a start, that he was talking to her.

Who could be ringing her? She felt confused and worried as she picked up the phone.

'Hello,' she whispered. 'Who is it?' she said a little louder.

'Kev.' It didn't tell her anything.

'You there Amy?' he sounded indignant.

'Yeeees.'

'Chrissie tells me you're not bothering with us now you've moved up.'

She had no idea what he was talking about – but she was meant to know, so she just said politely 'Does she?'

'Yeah, she does,' he sounded quite angry now.

'I'm sorry.' Perhaps he expected an apology.

'Sorry!' he exploded 'So it's true then.' The apology had obviously been a mistake and the phone at the other end was banged down.

'Amy! Don't forget it's Jimmy's morning at playschool tomorrow,' Dad called, 'and it's going to rain.' And she forgot about Kev and Chrissie, wondering why she had to remember about the playschool.

She took a mug of milk upstairs and found Jimmy sitting on the edge of his bed looking forlorn in pyjamas three sizes too big. She laughed and Danny and Aldous, coming in to the bedroom, laughed too.

'You look like a walrus,' Danny said. 'Clap your feet

together!' They all helped to roll up the sleeves and trouser legs then Jimmy said, 'I want Frog,' and the boys looked at Alice. She looked round the room desperately and saw a pile of books by the side of a cupboard but going through them she could see no sign of one about a frog.

'It's not here,' she said.

'It is.' Jimmy picked up the top book from the pile and waved it at her. *The Day the Fog Came*, it was called: she should have known.

Alice cleared her throat. She wasn't used to the sound of her own voice except when she read out loud, self-consciously, at school – pieces of poetry or prose in the English class.

She started in her usual, rather flat, monotonous tone without expression and was stopped by the sound of the boys' helpless laughter. 'Now do it properly,' Aldous said, 'like you always do.'

'Do all the voices,' Danny prompted.

A great feeling of tiredness suddenly came over her, 'My throat's a bit sore!' She tried another paragraph putting a bit more feeling into the words and then noticed, to her relief, that Jimmy was almost asleep. He reached up with his eyes nearly closed and gave her a hug. 'Love you,' he mumbled.

Alice couldn't remember anyone ever saying that to her before. She knew her parents must love her but they never said so. She hugged him to her – he was probably missing his mother. She felt as if she was going to cry.

'Good night,' she said quickly to Danny and Aldous.

'Night Amy – great cake,' Danny said.

She took the empty mug downstairs and caught sight of a laundry basket by the back door full of clothes waiting to be ironed, and she thought of the homework piled up on the table.

'You alright, Amy? You don't seem quite yourself this evening,' Dad looked up from a book he was reading.

*Not quite myself,* Alice thought wryly. She ought to tell them but how could she begin to explain – they'd think she'd gone mad. 'I'm okay,' was all she said. 'Think I'll go to bed now.'

'Done all your prep? It's important if you want to go to college like Thomas.' His eyes returned to his book but he continued talking. 'You're a good kid, Amy – the way you've managed while Mum's been away. Your Aunt Seely wanted to come and take over, but we've managed without her – thank goodness.' He looked at Alice and gave a big grin.

'Night Dad.'

Under the pillow on one of the beds in Amy's room she found a warm emerald green nightie. The other bed, which she hoped was Evalina's, had a satin nightdress in a peach colour draped over it.

She snuggled down under the flowered duvet.

In a funny way, she had never felt so happy. Would she wake up tomorrow and find she was back in her silent pale room again? Her mind was a kaleidoscope of brilliant colours. As she closed her eyes patterns of pink curtains, orange lights, yellow and turquoise whirled round to a background accompaniment of wild, unfamiliar music and strange rhythms.

# FOUR

Amy had leant forward to see if the orchid had a smell. She gripped one of the blooms with both hands and saw that the other girl was doing the same; she could hear her own family, noisy, behind her.

She breathed in deeply and looked into the spiralling design on the petals. A potent and unusual pepperminty smell came up to meet her and she could feel herself being drawn into the orchid, down, down. She felt as if she would never reach the end, then suddenly she was out into the open again, standing in the Tropical House but by herself now. Her family seemed to have gone without her, she was alone and it was silent; even the birds were quiet now.

She closed her eyes to enjoy the rare peace for a moment. *When I open them,* she thought, *they'll all be there again, arguing and shouting* – but they weren't.

*They'll have gone out the other way without me – they'll soon come running back, or perhaps they're hiding for a joke.* There was a slight movement behind a giant fern but it was only an elderly lady pushing it aside with her walking stick as she walked by.

No one seemed to be coming to look for her. It felt odd standing there by herself. She remembered Evalina saying something about tea. *They must have gone to the tea shop.* She stood for a minute by the exit to the Tropical House. It was getting dark outside now and very wet. She reached down to draw up the zip of her anorak but it wasn't there. A strange woman with a red umbrella and a cross expression on her face was bearing down on her.

'There you are,' she said, 'I've been waiting by the entrance door.' She grasped Amy by the shoulder. 'We'll have to get a taxi back home – I'm not waiting around for a bus in this weather.'

She had an air of such authority about her that Amy didn't question her. She must have somehow met up with the others and they'd all be waiting for her by the taxi rank.

They hurried along but before they reached the place where the taxis usually waited, the woman waved her umbrella at one coming round the corner: it came to an abrupt stop. Amy was propelled into the back seat and the woman said, 'Rosetti Grove.'

Everything had happened so quickly, Amy could hardly believe that she was hurtling through the wet, dark streets with someone she'd never seen before to an address she'd never heard of. She found her voice – 'Let me out, let me out of here!' and she banged on the window.

The woman looked startled, then angry. 'Stop doing that, whatever's the matter with you?'

They were stopped by some traffic lights and a street lamp outside illuminated the interior of the taxi.

'Help!' Amy tried the door – she was being kidnapped and she had to escape, but the woman caught hold of her hand.

'I don't know what game you're trying to play but it's a very childish one and look at the colour of your hands – chalk all over them – they're all the colours of the rainbow!'

Amy looked down but her hands to her looked white.

Instead of her anorak, she was wearing a pale brown coat and she wore slip-on shoes not her red trainers.

She sank back confused. 'Where are we going – who are you?' Even her voice was not her own: it was thinner, more high-pitched.

'Straight home and to bed in your case – you sound as if you've got a fever,' was the reply.

Catching sight of a face staring at her in the window, Amy stared back. It looked like the girl she'd seen in the Tropical House – pale and still. She reached out to touch it and the reflection reached back. With a startled shout of amazement she shrieked out, 'It's me!'

'That does it – the doctor for you, my girl.'

They had arrived at a row of small, thin, white stucco houses and the taxi drew up.

The woman looked grim as she paid the driver and then hauled Amy up the steps of number eleven. She fiddled with some keys and opened the door, and suddenly from the turmoil and upset of the taxi ride, Amy found herself in a haven of peace and tranquillity.

In a tiny corner of her mind, she had always imagined such a place and when the noise at home became too much she would try to switch it off and escape to this little oasis.

Light coloured walls and furnishings and soft lighting, nothing to disturb or jar the senses. She felt it must be wonderful to live in such an atmosphere as this.

A couple wearing similarly cream-coloured clothes came down the stairs in perfect harmony with the surroundings.

'There you are, Alice. Go and take your coat off and we'll have tea, and where are your slippers?' The woman, with very short hair, paused at the bottom of the stairs and frowned slightly at Amy's shoes.

'I think she's sickening for something,' the woman with the red umbrella looked accusingly at Amy. 'Behaved very oddly in the taxi – not quite herself.'

'Oh, she seems alright to me, Connie. By the way, are you going out tonight? The Ledgers have asked us to a private viewing of an exhibition – we're rather keen to go – post modernist.'

'Well... I...' Connie hesitated, but the man chipped in and her words were lost.

'How was the zoo? I'll take a look at your sketches over tea.'

Amy felt in her pocket and there was a small pad and some chalks. She wanted to say something but she'd have to think it out carefully. She found some slippers by the open door leading to a small white-painted cloakroom, and hung up her coat on a white coat hanger. There was a mirror over the washbowl and Amy stared at her reflection. She was certainly small and thin, with a pale face, light brown hair and greyish coloured eyes. A bit of brightening up would be a definite improvement. She washed her hands, taking care not to splash the small, neat watch on her wrist, and dried them on a fluffy beige towel. Reaching up to touch the straight, shiny hair she tried putting it behind her ears. *I wonder how I would look with Evalina's red wig,* she thought.

'Alice! Tea's ready – we haven't got all day!' the voice was coming from upstairs. *Do they take tea in the bedroom?* Amy wondered. She pushed open the door of the room next to the cloakroom and discovered a small tidy dining room with a glass-topped table. It smelt of polish and didn't look as if any meal had ever been enjoyed in it. Further down the hall, the kitchen door was open and Amy could see Connie cutting herself a large piece of cake. It suddenly reminded her of Danny and his birthday cake. She must say something right away.

She bounded up the waxed stairs two at a time and rushed into the sitting room where she could see the woman, who must be Alice's mother, pouring the tea.

'I'm not who you think I am,' she began in her new voice, which sounded timid and not nearly powerful enough. 'I'm someone else.'

'Terry's looking forward to seeing your sketches,' the woman said in an even tone, continuing to pour the tea.

Terry was tidying up the Sunday papers into a neat pile, then he re-arranged the cushions on the oatmeal coloured sofa, lit the gas fire and sat down in one of the uncomfortable looking grey chairs.

'Where are they then?' he asked Amy.

Her outburst had been totally ignored.

'Your sketches,' he persisted looking at his watch. He reached for his cup of tea and took a sip. 'Mmm very subtle, Bunny.'

'Camomile and blackcurrant,' she murmured.

Amy took the fragile bone china cup and saucer offered to her and tried again, 'Look, I'm not Alice – I don't know you. I don't live here and I haven't made any sketches.' The silence in the room seemed unearthly. Amy took a sip of the pale liquid in the cup. It was disgusting and tasted nothing like tea! She spat it out without realising what she was doing.

'Ughh – what is it?'

Terry breathed hard but his voice remained under control.

'I don't think you're quite yourself, are you?' he said through clenched teeth.

'That's just what I'm trying to tell you,' Amy said, hoping he'd realised that she was speaking the truth but he hadn't understood.

'Connie was right,' he said to Bunny, 'probably sickening for something.'

'I'm not so sure,' Bunny considered Amy for a moment, 'she could be striving to assert her inner subconscious personality. Nadia was only saying the other evening that Luke was going through a similar state of rebellion. She's read this marvellous book called *Mirror Disturbances of Identity Crises in the Young* – I must borrow it from her.'

They then both scrutinised Amy as if she were an

interesting curio in a museum. Then Bunny spoke. 'Sip your tea – they say it calms the nerves.'

Amy shrugged her shoulders. There was nothing more she could do at the moment. As soon as she had the chance, she'd ring home. She took a sip of the tea and wrinkled her nose again at the taste. Bunny and Terry exchanged a look of relief that her little outburst seemed to be over and that everything was back to normal.

'Interesting article in the paper here,' Terry tapped the *Sunday Reminder* with his hands, 'all about the importance of the vernacular in local architecture. See what you make of it. Oh and on page six, I've ringed a piece about amino acids.'

Amy took the paper and put down her cup and saucer. This was a subject she was very interested in. She glanced at the article. 'This theory's out of date – it's old hat. Dr Robinstein of Colorado University has written a new thesis on vegetables, where amino acids are missing.'

Terry's mouth opened but no words came out for a moment 'Well, yes... I suppose you could be right there. I do seem to remember... ' His voice tailed away but Amy wasn't listening anyway. At home, if she had a chance of reading the newspaper on a Sunday, the whole thing would have been crumpled and turned inside out by the time she got hold of it. It was a novelty to have it "as new" and she settled back to read.

Her brother, Thomas, training to be an accountant, was said to be the financial wizard in their family and often talked of stocks and shares and 'dabbling in the market.' She turned to the money page. 'I see Allport Thomson have gone public,' she said with surprise.

'Allport Thompson… Gone public,' Terry repeated in a bemused way.

'Bath time,' Bunny announced brightly looking at her watch. 'There's a programme on modern art in the U.K on television later. That'll be a treat, won't it? So good to expand one's visual concepts.'

*Visual concepts? What on earth was Bunny going on about now,* thought Amy. 'I'm hungry.' She suddenly realised she was ravenous; she thought of the chocolate cake she'd made – had it been eaten?

'Connie'll have your supper ready as usual after your bath!' Bunny followed Amy out of the room and said quietly, with a sad expression on her face, 'I think it was a little bit unfair of you to make a joke at Terry's expense. He puts a lot of hard work into your Sunday Newspaper Speculation time, you know.' And Amy was left feeling guilty without knowing why.

She wandered upstairs and discovered a beige painted bedroom, grey furniture, white bedspread. *Perhaps it's Connie's bedroom,* she thought, then she spotted a small white table with school books spread out all over it.

'The chief exports of Venezuela are…' she read in an open exercise book. She turned it over to see the name. ALICE FRASER. *That's who they think I am – Alice Fraser.*

There was absolute silence in the room. 'I'm Alice Fraser,' Amy said aloud, looking at herself in the mirror. She touched her straight smooth hair and looked at her grey eyes and small mouth. She tried to grin her usual big grin but it was now a tiny, tight smile. She couldn't remember any time when she'd been completely on her own like this – except in the bathroom and even then there was usually someone banging on the door to say 'Hurry up.' She closed her eyes and found herself enjoying the new experience; opening them again, she looked around. No mobile phone to be seen. She searched through tidy drawers and cupboards. No luck. *This'll make things tricky,* she thought. Going over to the window, she saw some activity in the street below. Boxes of books and lampshades were being carried from a car into the house next door. A boy of about her own age looked up at her window and she waved. Perhaps there were new people moving in.

She found the "all white" bathroom next to a room with a closed door and after she'd had a bath and washed her hair, drying it on white fluffy towels, she pinned her hair up on top of her head and went to see what was on the next landing.

The two rooms at the top of the house had been knocked into one and made into a studio. Turning on the lights, which were very bright, she saw they were angled on to two drawings boards; shelves of rolled up plans and books lined the room. There were a couple of computer screens and on top of a plans chest there was a large important-looking model of a building. So her "parents" were architects! Were they Alice's parents? If so, why were they referred to as Bunny and Terry?

Her stomach made a loud rumbling noise with hunger. She switched off the lights and ran downstairs two at a time. Pausing at the sitting room she stopped to listen but could hear nothing from behind the closed door. The peace and quiet of the house was beginning to affect her and she found herself creeping down to the kitchen.

The kitchen door was closed too, but behind it Amy could hear voices talking softly then suddenly an argument seemed to break out, which stopped abruptly as she opened the door.

Connie turned to face her, 'What are you doing down here? It's only half-past,' she said furiously.
The man she'd been talking to pushed past Amy. 'Next Friday, then.' He looked at Connie then let himself out of the front door quickly.

'Were you listening at the door?' Connie turned threateningly to Amy.

'No – I'm hungry – I'd like to get myself some supper.'

'Oh – you would, would you?' Connie's tone was sarcastic. 'Well, I think I can manage to organise the food in this house without any help from you, thank you very much.' And she went to a cupboard and reached up for a packet of cereal. She put it on the table with a jug of milk, bowl and spoon. 'There you are.' Her voice changed slightly and became more friendly. 'That was my young brother you saw just now – he's so good about keeping in touch – we were just having a laugh about the old days.'

Amy hadn't thought it sounded like that but she said nothing and polished off two wheat crunchies. 'What's next?' she asked.

Connie looked at her critically. 'What's *next*?' I thought you were sickening for something this afternoon,' she muttered darkly.

'I'm still hungry,' Amy persisted. She was used to good food and plenty of it.

'You can have a piece of bread and butter, I suppose,' Connie said grudgingly.

*So even the food here is beige,* Amy thought. 'I'll make some toast and open a tin of baked beans.'

'No beans.' Connie was scowling again now.

'Well, what is there then?' Amy went to open the cupboard but Connie barred her way.

'There's some raspberry jam here.' And she banged the pot down on the table and stood watching while Amy put some sliced bread in the toaster. A few crumbs on the white surface of the working top were quickly wiped away and as soon as Amy had finished her toast, her plates were whisked away and the kitchen restored to its immaculate condition.

'Well, they'll be waiting for you upstairs.' Connie looked at the clock on the wall.

*The house is run to a timetable,* Amy thought, and so it seemed, was Alice.

'Good night,' Connie dismissed her. Amy desperately wanted to find the telephone before Bunny and Terry should consult their watches and see it was time for the programme on "Modern art in the UK".

Thank goodness!

By the front door on a small piece of white grained marble was a flat cream-coloured telephone. She picked it up and quickly pressed her number at home. She didn't know what to say, her heart was pounding uncomfortably. They'd all be looking for her, wondering where she was – Mum would be upset. If she could just say… Someone picked up the phone the other end: there was noise in the background – jazz from the radio, a dog barking then Dad's voice, not very clear, 'Hello.'

What could she say. 'It's me – Amy.'

'Amy you want? Amy's in bed. I'll tell her you rang, who is it?'

Amy put down the phone. She'd expected to hear cries of relief not to hear that, 'Amy's in bed.' No one was worried; Dad was playing his jazz and "Amy" was in bed.

She sat on the bottom stair feeling puzzled and bewildered. Then in a flash she realised what must have happened. *I'm Alice and she's me. We've swapped places for some reason. But we haven't exchanged entirely. Deep inside myself, I'm still me. It's only a part-exchange.*

She thought back to the Tropical House and remembered thinking that it would be nice to be Alice – so quiet and calm – and now she *was* Alice.

Well, nobody was worried about her, that was certain. She'd got her wish and perhaps she ought to make the most of it – it may only last for twenty-four hours and then she'd be Amy Formica again in the middle of her noisy, intrusive family.

She licked away some raspberry jam from the corner of her mouth and went up the wax polished stairs to the sitting room and one of the uncomfortable grey armchairs, prepared to widen her visual concepts, as Bunny would say.

# FIVE

A bell was clanging somewhere near her head and Alice sat up in alarm, wondering where she was. A light was switched on and she saw bright walls and colourful curtains. Someone in the next bed was groaning loudly.

Everything clicked into place and she realised she was still in the house in Disraeli Drive: still Amy Formica.

Evalina groaned again and sat up, 'Dawn of another lovely day.' She yawned.

There was noise outside on the landing and the sound of taps running and doors banging.

It was all so different from the lonely silence of her own room, and Alice sat still for a moment enjoying the companionable noises. A radio was switched on somewhere and Evalina was now shouting to her, something about some ironing Amy had promised to do.

'No, I haven't done it.' Alice had never done any ironing. She didn't think Bunny had either.

'You promised!' Evalina screamed. 'You know I needed that shirt today. I'm going to ask for my rise. I've been at Frudents for a year now. If I don't get it, I'll leave and get a job in the city, plenty of good secretarial jobs going there *or* I may decide on a change… become a model perhaps.'

She had put on a satin wrap and was studying herself in the mirror. Her voice was wheedling now. 'You could do it before breakfast, couldn't you? There's a love.' And she went to see if the bathroom was free.

Alice found a school shirt in a chest of drawers and a navy skirt hanging up in a wardrobe dominated by some of Evalina's glamorous assortment of clothes. She hoped she had picked the right colours for the school she'd be expected to attend. It couldn't be worse than Huxley House – it might even be better. At the back of her mind, she knew she should ring home and say something to her parents but she was swept along in the morning rush – *I'll do it later,* she told herself.

There seemed to be a fight going on in the boys' room and the noise had started the dog barking: the whole house seemed to be vibrating with sound.

Breakfast was very different to the cup of mint tea and a piece of toast and marmalade that Alice was used to, usually eaten in a tense silence. Dad had already gone off to work – she still hadn't puzzled out what he did – but the others, one by one, gathered round the large table and helped themselves to great bowls of cereal and milk, baked beans on toast and Aldous was making a fry up for himself consisting of sausages, bacon and egg all sizzling together in a large frying pan. Evalina, still in her satin wrap, said she was on a new diet so had orange juice, a grapefruit and a lightly boiled egg. Alice tucked in with relish but eating more slowly. Soon Aldous and Danny had finished and rushed off to school. Jimmy fixed his large dark eyes on her expectantly. She remembered the remark about 'playschool'. Where was it? And where was her own school?

'Don't forget my shirt, will you?' Evalina pleaded, 'and there's all that washing to take down to the launderette.'

There didn't seem to be a minute to think. Uncle Edgar popped his head round the back door 'Coffee. Run out of coffee,' he explained and helped himself to a jar from the cupboard. He looked up at Alice 'What's the matter girl – you look perplexed?'

She shook her head. 'The ironing, playschool… launderette…'

There was a look of concern in his eyes and he stopped grinning for a minute. He looked at the clock. 'Where's the ironing?' They both looked round and spotted a pink plastic basket on top of a cupboard. 'Leave it to me,' he said cheerfully.

Alice felt relieved – she wanted everything to go smoothly for as long as she was part of the family.

Uncle Edgar was whistling his tune "Streetwise", while he deftly put up the ironing board. Jimmy was tugging at Alice's skirt. 'Where…?' she began and didn't know how to go on. How could she ask where her school was – and the playschool?

The back door opened again.

'Hi Chrissie,' Uncle Edgar said cheerfully. 'You two are going to be late again.'

'Well come on,' Chrissie said to Alice impatiently.

She was a girl of about her own age – tall with a sulky expression, wearing an anorak, a school bag slung over her shoulder. 'I suppose we've got to drop you off, have we?' she said to Jimmy. Alice grabbed the anorak she'd worn yesterday and followed Chrissie gratefully – the launderette would have to wait.

They hurried along through a maze of damp streets. They passed a telephone box and Alice thought guiltily about Bunny and Terry. She'd managed to take a quick look at the *Mercury* over the breakfast table and had seen no headlines about herself – no "Girl missing after zoo visit", but she had no time to think any more about it as Jimmy was suddenly clinging to her. 'Don't want to go.'

'Come on, in you go,' Chrissie said bossily as she rang a door bell at a large terrace house.

A motherly woman appeared and picked Jimmy up, smiling – 'How's your mother getting on?' she asked Alice.

'Alright thank you,' Alice said rather awkwardly.

'She'll be in hospital for two weeks and then she'll have to rest up – she's had slight complications,' Chrissie said with authority 'Mum says you have to be careful with varicose veins.'

This sounded like one of Aunt Seely's pronouncements – perhaps Chrissie was her "cousin".

Jimmy seemed happier now and the girls rushed off down to the main road where suddenly hundreds of other boys and girls were converging on a huge, red brick modern building, spread out over two or three acres, like a giant Lego model.

For a second Alice took fright – what was she doing

here – she wouldn't know any of the people or any of the work she was supposed to know. She'd say she felt ill and escape somehow. But she felt the steely grip of Chrissie's fingers on her arm.

'Kev wants to see you at lunch.' She looked hostile. 'Look, we all know how brainy you are being shoved up to 8A but you don't need to put on airs and avoid all your friends. It's not very nice for me, see?'

Alice looked at her without understanding. 'What?'

'Oh don't come the innocent with me – you can hardly bring yourself to speak to us these days.'

Chrissie suddenly caught sight of some of her friends and went over to them, linking arms and went off with them, giggling.

Alice was left abandoned in the entrance hall, full of noise and shouting, pushing and shoving with corridors going off in different directions. Someone she took to be a master swooped down on her. 'You've been moved up to 8A and my little lot I hear. Congratulations. Ambitions in the scientific direction I gather,' he shouted. Alice's heart sank. Science was her worst subject.

She followed him down passages and up stairs, and found herself at last in a large airy classroom full of desks, most of them occupied. She slipped into one near the front. *I'll just keep quiet and lie low,* she thought to herself.

It was all very different to Huxley House. Here there was a relaxed atmosphere. Bob Pierce, bearded and sandaled, taking the register, joked with the class and Alice was able to muddle through his history class where there was lively discussion on concepts of constitution. In the French lesson they acted a small play instead of learning their verbs parrot fashion. She produced a large splashy picture of a fabric design in art and by then it was lunch time and she'd found she'd enjoyed the morning.

She followed the others down to the dining hall and stood in a queue with a tray. She saw Chrissie at the far table talking and laughing with friends. She was dug sharply in the back with a tray and looked round.

'Some of us are going to the Ice Rink on Saturday, want to come or are you too high and mighty for us now?' A boy with dark untidy hair was scowling at her. Was he a friend of Amy's? Across the room, Alice could see Chrissie beckoning to him to come and join them, while she was being ignored.

'Are you going to come or not?' he persisted. It seemed to be some sort of ultimatum.

'My mother's in hospital, it's a bit difficult...' she didn't know what to say.

'That's just an excuse – Chrissie says...'

Alice was trying to put two and two together. Amy was popular and clever, she'd moved up into a higher division and Chrissie was spreading the rumour that she was now too stuck up to see her old friends. Chrissie was perhaps jealous and maybe not only of her academic achievements but of her friendship with Kev.

She smiled Amy's big friendly smile and said, 'I'll really try to get along.' She couldn't ice skate and had no idea where the rink was but felt she owed it to Amy to keep things going. Kev looked pleased and grinned.

A girl from her class with fluffy fair hair asked Alice

to join her at her table and when they had started their pasty and baked beans, she pulled a long face. 'Ugh – Science this afternoon. I hate it.'

'So do I,' said Alice without thinking.

'You can't hate it – you're meant to be brilliant at it – that's why you moved up, isn't it?'

'Oh… well,' Alice hurriedly tried to look modest, 'I don't like it all the time, some of it's alright.'

'I can't stand any of it. Can I work with you and you can help me?' she stabbed her fork into a piece of pastry.

'Well… yes,' but Alice thought she might be the one in greater need of help and wondered again if she could somehow escape but her new friend, Debbie, stuck firmly by her side until it was time for afternoon lessons.

The science room smelt of bad eggs and bonfires and Miss Thwaite, with horn-rimmed spectacles and white overalls, was busy with Bunsen burners and test tubes and measuring liquids from coloured bottles.

'Right– choose partners – we're going to do an experiment with potassium permanganate this afternoon.' Her voice was brisk and authoritative and her eye fastened on Alice.

'Ah – Amy Formica – I've had some good reports of your work from Mr Johnstone.'     Alice said nothing. 'Come and work over at this bench.' She indicated one in a prominent position. 'Who are you working with?'

Debbie pushed forward. 'With me.'

Miss Thwaite smiled a thin smile. 'Well perhaps you'll learn something for a change.'

She described the experiment and quickly drew some complicated diagrams on the blackboard which they were meant to copy into their exercise books. Debbie nudged Alice and shrugged her shoulders. 'She's lost me completely. Hope you're getting it all down,' and she drew a paperback romantic novel out of a pocket and, putting it on her knee, became engrossed in her story.

'And now before we set up our experiment,' Miss Thwaite smiled brightly at her class, 'we're going to use some magnesium ribbon. I told you all about it last week. We're going to see what happens when we light a little.' She cast her eye around and it fastened on Alice. 'You can assist me.' She spoke as if she was conveying a great honour.

'I will light the Bunsen burner and you can cut off some ribbon. It's over there – ' she pointed to a cupboard '– and light it, holding it carefully in these tongs.'

She busied herself setting up the Bunsen burner and answered the questions of a boy standing near by. With sinking heart, Alice opened the cupboard.

Inside, among phials and bottles, she saw a spool of white metal ribbon. She stretched some out. It was lightweight and she guessed she would need to cut off quite a good length for it to take any effect. She snipped off about 30 centimetres and, holding it with the tongs, plunged it straight into the burner.

A great white sheet of flame leapt up lighting the whole classroom with a dazzling brightness. Miss Thwaite screamed and panic broke out.

Someone opened a window and Alice, who had somehow managed to hold on to the burning ribbon, dropped it out of the window where it fell through the air accompanied by a trail of smoke.

Test tubes and retorts had been knocked over, and a large glass jar containing green crystals had been smashed as everyone had pushed towards the classroom door.

'Thank you, Amy,' Miss Thwaite said sarcastically. Everyone was coughing with the smoke, eyes streaming. 'Class dismissed.'

Alice caught a brief glimpse through the fog of Miss Thwaite's ferocious smile. 'I'll see you later,' she promised, then was seized by a fit of choking.

'I'll help clean up,' Alice offered, appalled at the chaos she'd caused but just at that moment a loud clanging bell was heard ringing out with a deafening noise. It was the fire alarm.

Immediately everyone formed into orderly lines and, trying not to run, moved swiftly through corridors, down stairs and out into the freezing air outside, where an anxious head teacher was trying to calm the excited ranks, and looking all the time for signs of flames licking round the building.

'Who set off the alarm?'

'Someone said the whole kitchen's on fire.'

'No, it's the gym.'

Everyone seemed to have their own opinion and the talk was noisy and excited. Anything for a change from the usual boring routine was welcome.

'Quiet everyone!' the voice of Mrs Craig, the head, came through a loud hailer now but had little effect on the babble.

Alice, watching quietly, saw Miss Thwaite appear, smudged and dishevelled, whispering something to Mrs Craig who put her hand up for silence. 'It appears there has been some mistake,' she shouted grimly, 'it has been a false alarm – apparently there has been a-a-an unfortunate incident in the science laboratory causing a disturbance.'

So that was it. The smoke alarm must have been activated. All heads in 8A swivelled to look at Alice who wished she could sink through the ground. To think that she had disrupted the whole school like this, she who was always so reserved and quiet at school, always timid and hating to draw attention to herself; she, whose school reports read, "Alice must learn to be more assertive". Well, she had certainly asserted herself this time. When she looked up, she saw that her classmates were grinning – one patted her on the back and someone else said, 'Good old Amy – there's always a bit of action when she's around.' They probably thought she'd caused the commotion on purpose. Perhaps Amy did those sort of things, so instead of trying to hide behind someone she gave a smile and shrugged her shoulders.

It was starting to rain heavily – Dad had been right about the weather.

'Back to your classrooms quickly,' came the order and there was more confusion and jostling as everyone made their way back into school.

Games were off because of the rain but in the gym, Alice found she was more agile than usual and was able to keep her balance walking along the bar – perhaps she'd even be able to ice-skate! She realised with a shock that she was thinking about Saturday and that maybe she'd be back in Rosetti Grove by then and all this would feel like just a dream. But she wasn't ready to go back yet – she was enjoying life as Amy Formica.

During the last lesson of the day, English, 8A joined up with 8B. Alice followed the others and found herself in a large classroom with Chrissie glaring at her from the back, sitting next to Kev who had saved a place for her in front of him. Chrissie was too quick and beckoned to another of her friends to sit there and Alice was forced to sit in the front row again.

The others had all learned a poem and were asked to recite it in turn by Mr Cox: ginger haired and short tempered. Alice was nervous; she could feel Chrissie's hostile eyes burning into her back. She'd never heard this poem before but she had learnt some passages from Shakespeare at Huxley House. Long chunks by heart and most of it making very little sense.

The boy sitting next to her had stammered his way through "Buttercups" accompanied by laughter and sarcastic comments from the others, and he sat down with relief.

'You!' It was Alice's turn.

'I did some Shakespeare instead,' she mumbled.

'Speak up.'

'I learnt some *Julius Caesar* instead.'

'Oh – you did, did you?'

The class went quiet and waited in anticipation for another piece of action from Amy.

She stood up.

'Friends, Romans, Countrymen…'

She was getting used to her new voice now and it was a very suitable one for Mark Anthony's speech. She spoke out, slowly, powerfully and there was a moment's silence when she finished, then someone started clapping.

'Yes, well, not the work I set you to do but... not bad, not bad at all. We'll have to see about getting a part for you in the play next term.'

Alice felt pleased that she hadn't let Amy down this time and gathered her things together ready to go home. She wondered if she'd be able to find her way back to Disraeli Drive but Chrissie was waiting for her in the cloakroom.

'What d'you want to go and show off like that in English for? It was really embarrassing,' she said angrily.

Alice didn't reply and they set off through the darkening streets in the rain. She wondered if she was expected to buy some food for supper and she remembered someone mentioning the launderette. If she had a moment to herself, she must ring Bunny and try to explain...

She turned into the gate of number six and turned to say 'goodbye' to Chrissie.

'Weren't you meant to be collecting Jimmy?' Chrissie shouted and was gone.

She hadn't realised. She raced back along the street and tried to remember the way to the large terrace house where they'd left him that morning, but she couldn't find it again. Half sobbing, she re-traced her steps to Disraeli Drive and ran up to the backdoor, flinging it open. She didn't know how she could explain it.

Uncle Edgar was sitting at the kitchen table pouring out a cup of tea, and next to him was Jimmy.

'I told Chrissie I'd collect him today, didn't she tell you?' Uncle Edgar said, seeing her astonishment. 'Come and have some tea, and I've fed the dog for you too, and the birds.'

It was warm and relaxing in the kitchen. Aldous and Danny weren't back yet nor was Dad.

'Hope Evalina's got that pay rise, otherwise there'll be fireworks.' Uncle Edgar pulled a face as he buttered some toast. 'Did you get anything for supper tonight?'

Alice shook her head.

'Well, it's just as well I bought a couple of pizzas.'

Alice thought she'd better start keeping lists like her mother. There seemed so much to remember. 'Thanks for doing the ironing,' she said.

Uncle Edgar gave a little mock bow. 'No problem – I was trying to think of some words for the last bit of "Streetwise", it goes like this.' And he sang again the tune he'd played last night. 'It's going round and round in my brain but I can't get the words to fit: can you take some of my clothes when you go to the launderette?' he said suddenly coming back to earth.

Alice had noticed a telephone box by a brightly lit launderette nearby and after she'd had a quick cup of tea, she gathered up any clothes she found lying around on the bedroom floor and in the bathroom, and went off to see if Uncle Edgar had any change for the washing machines.

'Dip into the B Fund as usual,' he said mysteriously.

'Where is it?' she asked without thinking.

'If it hasn't walked, it's in the usual place, of course, on top of the bookcase.'

Alice stood on a chair in the sitting room and reached up to a wooden box. It wasn't very heavy and, placing it on an armchair, she saw that the top was covered in a collage of post-cards showing tropical islands: turquoise sea, palm trees and coral beaches.

'What's the latest count?' Uncle Edgar lifted the lid of the box and they both peered inside at all the bank notes and some silver. There was a small piece of paper stuck into a rubber band round one of the piles of notes and on it was written – £557.50.

Alice had never seen so much money gathered together.

'Five hundred and fifty-seven pounds and fifty pence... well – your Mum and Dad will soon be able to take that magic holiday over the seas and far away.' He flicked through the notes with a dreamy look in his eyes. 'It pays to save – it pays, pays to save.' He liked the sound of the words and tapped out the rhythm on the box lid then handed some of the silver to Alice, took a pencil from behind his ear and adjusted the amount on the piece of paper. 'Every little windfall helps – the change from your Dad's pocket and even those empty bottles I took back – we just want another premium bond win now, eh?' He popped the lid back on the box and Alice went to find a bin liner bag for the pile of washing.

'Aren't you going to use Jimmy's old buggy?' Uncle Edgar asked as he saw her struggling.

'Oh yes of course.'

Jimmy pushed it out of the cloakroom for her.

A young woman at the launderette showed her how to work the switches of the machine and where to put the washing powder.

'Very, very hot please,' Alice said thinking that would be best and bundled the whole lot in.

While it was swirling round she tried to think about

what she was going to say to Bunny on the telephone but her thoughts were disturbed suddenly.

'Hi, Amy'!

Two girls about the same age as Alice banged on the window of the launderette and waved. Then they came in.

'See you at Des's party tonight – should be great,' one of them shouted over the noise of the machines.

*This is dreadful,* thought Alice. They must be Amy's friends and she was meant to be going out with them to some party, goodness knows where. Well, she'd have to say no.

'Sorry, I can't make it.'

'But you said… Jess, didn't she say…'

The other girl nodded her head.

'Something's come up – family stuff.'

'Family stuff? What family stuff?'

Alice thought frantically. Remembering her own packed timetable at home, she blurted out 'I have to take Aldous to his flute class… Danny to his clay modelling and oil painting lessons… and Jimmy has origami,' she finished with a flourish.

The two girls looked amazed.

'Jimmy has origami,' Jess repeated weakly. 'What's that? Sounds painful.'

'It's Japanese – cutting objects out of paper – very complicated.'

'I thought he was only three.'

'He's a sort of child prodigy.'

There was a silence while they took this in.

'Well, if you're not coming to Des's can I borrow

that top you wore when we went to Kev's?' Jess asked.

'Sorry. Evalina borrowed it,' Alice improvised. 'It got burnt in a fire and there's a huge hole in it.'

Jess made a face. 'Come on, Casey.'

Casey hesitated, remembering something. 'We've lost your mobile number,' she said to Alice. She fished in a pocket for a scrap of paper. 'Right, fire away.'

Alice felt in her pockets for Amy's mobile but there wasn't one. She racked her brains. 'I'm getting a new one. I lost my old one when I went to the opera.'

Jess and Casey looked at each other. Opera!

'Stuck up or what?' Jess muttered.

'Yeah, maybe Chrissie was right… She's got her mind on higher things these days.'

They gave a nasty laugh and went out.

*I think I've made enemies of those two. Sorry, Amy,* Alice said to herself, *but I got away with it.*

Her eye was caught by the soggy clothes whirling round slowly as the washing machine completed its cycle, then she had to ask for help to get them out. She stuffed the whole lot back into the bin liner, lugged it on to the buggy and set off for the telephone kiosk with a thudding heart.

What on earth was she going to say to Bunny? How could she begin to explain that she had somehow jumped into someone else's skin, her life, her family and had become someone completely different *but* in one way had stayed herself? Well she had to try.

She put her money in with shaking fingers and pressed her number, holding her breath.

While it rang, her thoughts raced… What must have

happened when Connie wasn't able to find her at the zoo? Her parents must be desperate but... Then suddenly there was Bunny herself answering.

'Bunny – it's me – it's Alice.' But the voice was Amy's and after a moment's silence Bunny replied sharply.

'Who is this?'

'It's me – Alice – I'm quite safe but...'

'Is this some kind of joke – because if so it's rather childish and very unfunny.'

With a huge effort Alice tried to make her voice sound more like her own.

'This is Alice.'

'I happen to be extremely busy. Now please stop wasting my time,' and Bunny rang off.

Alice put back the receiver and closed her eyes. This was horrible. She hadn't expected this reaction from her mother... there was no warmth, no enormous relief... or even interest. Didn't they care that she'd vanished? Didn't they want her back? She felt panic and a terrible desolation.

Someone was banging impatiently on the side of the kiosk, a car horn sounded loudly. She opened her eyes, went out in a daze and trundled the buggy down the road trying to think clearly.

*Why* wasn't Bunny worried and why hadn't she been missed? How could she think it was just a joke? Unless... she suddenly remembered the way Amy's family had accepted her quite naturally from the moment she'd made her wish. Was it possible that Amy had jumped into *her* skin and become Alice? Had they changed places and was Amy now living at Rosetti Grove with Bunny and Terry and going to Huxley House? That would explain Bunny's lack of concern. All she had to do, she told herself, was to wish hard enough and everything would be back to normal again any time she wanted. Inside, deep down, she was still herself – still Alice Fraser, it was only a swap over...

She had reached Disraeli Drive – it felt like her home now. The lights were on in the sitting room and in the bedroom she shared with Evalina.

The buggy squeaked noisily as she pushed it to the back door. The dog started barking. She was just wondering how Amy was enjoying being her – and what about Zelda – when Dad opened the door and helped her in with the washing. He was off to visit Mum in hospital.

'Any messages for her?' he asked. 'How have you got on in your new class – manage the work okay?'

Alice's mind flickered back over the science class. Better keep quiet about that. 'I may be chosen for a part in a play,' she said hesitantly.

'That's great.' Dad gave a smile as big as Amy's own. 'We'll all come and see it.'

There was a lovely smell of pizza in the kitchen where Uncle Edgar was trying out his new tune again.

'Ready in five minutes,' he sang. 'Mushroom pizzas ready in fi-i-i-ve minutes.'

Aldous and Danny were lying on the carpet in the sitting room engrossed in a loud space film on television – their hair still damp from a session at the swimming club.

'Don't forget to do your homework,' Dad called over

all the noise before he went out banging the door. The boys took no notice, lost in a world of a science fiction adventure.

Alice collected her school books and went upstairs.

Evalina was painting her fingernails in short angry strokes to the accompaniment of some beat music and watched by Jimmy.

'There you are.' She looked up briefly as Alice came in. 'Have you seen my wig? I want to wear it this evening. Haven't been trying it on, have you? I've warned you about that.'

Alice shook her head while Evalina continued to scowl. The music finished and now the telephone could be heard ringing.

'Well answer it, can't you – you can see my nails are wet.'

'Hallo…' she could hardly hear her own voice above the noise. 'Could you speak louder please.'

'Hallo – is that Amy?' the voice over the line was faint. 'It's Thomas.'

'Speak up.'

'I can't. Someone might hear. Look – I'm in big trouble. I need your help. Meet me at Penny Whistle – five o'clock tomorrow evening *but don't tell a soul.* I'm…' There was a click.

'Hello!' she shouted, her heart thumping, but he'd rung off.

# SIX

'Come and get it!' Uncle Edgar's voice sang out from the kitchen.

For a minute the house was a little quieter as Evalina's music had stopped and the boys switched off the television set, then the noise started up again. The boys chased each other, pushing and shouting, to the kitchen and Evalina was shrieking something about her wig, as she came downstairs. 'Have you been to the launderette?' she asked Alice. 'I want my green shirt tonight – you'll iron it for me won't you, after supper?'

Where or what or who was Penny Whistle, Alice wondered. She was supposed to know... Supposed to meet someone she didn't know tomorrow evening at an unknown place. Well, perhaps she just wouldn't turn up. But she knew Amy would go and help Thomas if he was in trouble and now it seemed she *was* Amy. There seemed to be so many things to think about and no time or peace to think things out quietly.

'I said when did you last see my red wig?' Evalina kicked Alice's foot impatiently under the table. 'What's got into you – you look as if you're only half there most of the time?'

Alice came to with a start. 'I haven't seen it since last night.'

'Take no notice of her.' Uncle Edgar caught Alice's eye and gave the "thumbs down" sign. 'She didn't get her rise at Frudents so she's taking it out on everyone.'

Evalina pushed her chair back from the table. 'I told them I'd be handing in my notice tomorrow. I'm tired of sitting at an office desk. Fruit flavoured toothpaste... huh! Forget it! I'm up for a career change. I'm going to work as a model.' She frowned at Aldous and Danny who were laughing exaggeratedly at her announcement. 'Alright, you can laugh but a friend of Paul's knows someone who works on *New World* magazine and I'm going to meet him this evening.' She would have flounced out of the room dramatically but Aldous shouted, 'Your turn to do the washing up.'

The handle of the back door rattled, the dog barked and Aunt Seely came into the kitchen and settled her large weight into a chair, when she'd taken off her coat and scarf. There was no mention of Aldous and the jug of water.

'Just doing my duty – I promised your mother I'd keep an eye on you while she was in hospital.' She eyed the remains of the pizza and fruit pie with seeming disapproval but helped herself to what was left.

'Chrissie's busy with her homework,' she said looking critically at Alice while Evalina banged about angrily among some of the crockery, stacking it up to drain.

'I'm going to see your poor mother tomorrow evening…' Aunt Seely had to shout above the noise from the sink and the words 'poor mother' made Jimmy suddenly start to cry.

'Right – that's it – I've done my share,' Evalina said, 'where's my green shirt?' she looked at Amy and her voice became a shade softer, 'Just time for you to press it while I go and get myself ready.'

'Where are you off to?' Aunt Seely asked.

'If you must know, I'm going to meet someone about a job in modelling – you know – photographs, magazines, clothes…'

'You don't mean you're giving up that good job at Frudent?'

'I certainly do.'

Alice had forgotten about the black bin liner full of washing, which lay by the door and she went over to look for the green shirt, wondering why Evalina couldn't iron it herself.

She started to pull out the garments putting them on the end of the table.

Out came: two pairs of pale green pants, a large vest of Dad's with artistic streaks of lime green, a multi-coloured towel, a couple of T-shirts with strange designs of green…

The talking at the table died away and all eyes were on Alice as she produced the next article like a magician taking a rabbit out of his hat.

'My T-shirts – they look great – how did you do it?' Aldous shouted.

'Look at Dad's vest!'

Jimmy's pyjamas and a couple of school shirts also seemed to have undergone a sea change. The boys were laughing. Evalina sat very quiet, her eyes riveted on the bag. Other clothes were recognised by the owners and Uncle Edgar identified Dad's best cream-coloured shirt now decorated with delicate touches of the same pale green.

Alice reached down deep into the bin liner and came up with a small shirt – dark green and shrivelled – she waited for Jimmy to claim it but there was a sudden piercing scream from Evalina.

'Oh no! I don't believe it! My shirt, brand new – what have you done to it?'

Alice couldn't believe it was Evalina's. She dipped down again and brought out a curiously stiff blue cardigan – shrunken and felt-like – which no one wanted to recognise as their own.

'Oh dear, oh dear.' Aunt Seely shook her head sadly from side to side. 'This is a catastrophe – whatever will your mother say – whatever possessed you?'

'I just put all the clothes into the machine and pressed the "very hot" programme and…'

'All "very hot"?' Evalina shrieked. 'Didn't you bother to read the label "wash separately, cool wash" it says. I think you've done this on purpose haven't you?'

'No honestly I…'

The boys were doubled up –

'More, more,' Danny gasped.

Alice hardly liked to see if there was anything else left – she put her hand down and withdrew it again quickly. 'Ugghh!' There was something down there but it felt like an animal with damp fur. Surely she hadn't put a cat into the machine, it was a terrible thought.

'What is it – what is it?' Jimmy was chanting – he looked happy now, it was like opening a Christmas stocking.

Nervously Alice reached down and her fingers closed round the object – it felt horrible. Hardly daring to look, she drew it out very gingerly and held it up. It didn't bear any resemblance to anything any of them had ever seen and they all looked at it in wonder.

Greeny-gold, hairy, lank and damp, it hung for a minute then Alice dropped it on to the table, screwing up her face in distaste. Even Evalina was quiet, then she let out another scream – far louder even than her last one.

'Shut up – you'll frighten the neighbours.' Uncle Edgar looked quite frightened himself.

'My wig!' she cried. 'It's ruined – ruined.'

They stared in amazement at the forlorn looking heap on the table.

'No – your wig's red,' Danny said in disbelief, but Aunt Seely nodded her head sagely.

'That's what it is, sure enough – the colour from the green shirt's run into everything and…'

Evalina sobbed with rage while Uncle Edgar rocked from side to side, tears of laughter pouring down his cheeks; Danny and Aldous fought to try on the wig and Jimmy had the hiccups.

'Evalina – I'm sorry, really…' Alice didn't know what to say but, gathering up her dignity, Evalina stormed from the room leaving her shirt and wig behind and slammed the door loudly.

'I just picked everything up from the bedroom floor in a bundle.' Alice tried to remember gathering up the washing.

'You've done it this time,' Aunt Seely said grimly. 'Poor Evalina.' She looked at Alice with large, sad eyes. 'She has every right to be so upset – I just don't know what's got into you, nearly setting the school on fire, poisoning that cake… and with your mother in hospital too. How are you going to make it up to your sister?'

'C'mon, Seely, it's not that bad.' Uncle Edgar made an effort at recovering himself and dabbed at his eyes with a large spotted handkerchief. 'We can repay her from the B Fund – we always use it for emergencies…' He broke off again as Aldous had plonked the wig on his head at a rakish angle… 'a little more to the right I think.'

'Your poor parents will never get their holiday in Barbados at this rate –' but no one was taking much notice of her – the boys wanted Alice to tell them about the "fire".

'Doesn't anyone ever make a cup of coffee round here?' Aunt Seely snapped, fixing her eye on Alice. 'A good strong cup.'

Alice put the kettle on. She wasn't sure how to make coffee – they only drank tea at home: herbal or weak china tea. She found a jar of instant coffee. *How many spoonfuls*, she wondered. She put in four. *And why doesn't Aunt Seely go home and get Chrissie to make her a cup?*

'And when are you going to get a proper job instead of sitting around here all day?' Aunt Seely was fixing her mournful attention on Uncle Edgar now. 'Strumming that guitar won't get you anywhere.' She sighed. 'It seems to me that Thomas is the only one with...' she took the cup that Alice handed to her and took a sip: she shuddered. 'Poisonous! Don't you think you've done enough mischief for one day?' She glared at Alice and heaved herself out of her seat slowly, putting on her coat and scarf while Aldous, with exaggerated politeness, opened the back door for her. 'I'll look in tomorrow evening, after I've been to visit your mother,' she said ominously and vanished into the dark.

The boys returned to the television.

'What can I do about all this?' Alice asked Uncle Edgar in despair.

'Don't worry about it. Evalina should do her own washing anyway. I've got to go down to the launderette with some more of my own things. I'll take them and use a specially strong powder and with a bit of luck, it should bleach the colour out. All the same,' he looked at Alice quizzically, 'it's not like you to get it so wrong or *did* you do it on purpose?'

'No – I didn't – I was in a rush and...'

'Alright, alright... and in return for doing the washing you can help me to finish my song.' He went through to the sitting room to fetch his guitar.

Soon it would be time to put Jimmy to bed. She hadn't even opened a page of her homework and now she was expected to do some song-writing. She sighed and for a brief moment thought of her quiet life at Rosetti Grove and the peace of her own room there. Then the telephone rang. It was someone wanting to bring round a sick cat for Dad's advice.

Uncle Edgar plugged in his guitar and played a couple of chords. 'It's about this guy swaggering down the City Street, putting on a big act for the benefit of his friends.

*When it's hot on the street*
*And he starts to feel the beat*
*Kicks the litter round his feet*
    *He's sure he's very cool*
    *And Streetwise*

*The buzzing of the flies*
*Neon lights flash in his eyes*
*The City is his prize*
    *He's sure he's very cool*
    *And Streetwise*

*Well who's he going to cheat*
*In the dust and the heat*
*The "big act" ain't so sweet*
    *He's sure he's very cool*
    *And Streetwise*

*Buildings hide the midnight skies*
*Roaring traffic drowns his lies –*'

He came to an abrupt stop and shrugged his shoulders.

'What about... "Big talk, big buys"...' Alice suggested tentatively.

'I like it. I like it – yeah...' he grinned.

*'Buildings hide the midnight skies*
*Roaring traffic drowns his lies*
*Big talk... Big buys...*

Mmm, nearly there. Thanks, Amy, you're a star!'
'I'll try to think of a last line,' she promised.

They heard Evalina come downstairs and slam the front door as she went out. The sick cat arrived in a basket, then Dad arrived home looking worried – Mum hadn't been feeling so good today.

After settling Jimmy down and reading to him, Alice went to fetch her school books. Evalina had left their bedroom in a dreadful mess – however did Amy ever manage to do any homework? She felt tired and found it impossible to concentrate on the page she was meant to be reading. Her mind dwelt gloomily on all that had happened that day – she'd brought the school to a standstill, ruined lots of clothes, not to mention an expensive wig, upset Aunt Seely and she hadn't found out about Penny Whistle yet.

She heard a step on the stairs and the door of her room opened. Quickly she pretended to be engrossed in her book. A hand patted her on the shoulder.

'I hear you've had quite a day.' Dad was looking down at her with a twinkle in his eye. He looked round the room. 'We could use a bit more space, couldn't we? It's a pity you can't work in the caravan like Thomas used to but while Edgar...'

More space, that sounded like something Bunny or Terry might talk about, their speciality used to be conversions and extensions. What would they advise, she wondered.

'The loft,' she said knowing from the height of the roof that there must be one, 'what about the loft? We could turn it into another room!'

'You know, you may have something there. Mind you, it would cost a lot.'

'Not if you have a friend who could help – we could do it more or less for the price of the materials – we'd need floor joists, boarding, some plasterboard and insulation – oh and a loft ladder and a window or roof light.'

Dad looked astonished. 'How on earth do you know all that?'

'Oh – I – just picked it up.' She'd absorbed more than she'd realised living with two architects all her life.

'Well, we'll think about it. It might be a very good idea. Somewhere to go for a bit of peace and quiet – a hideaway – and of course it would add value to the house. Edgar's got that friend in the building trade.' He went out but paused for a moment by the door. 'There might be some fog about tomorrow – muffle up and straight home from school.'

*He seems very knowledgeable about the weather,* Alice thought, *perhaps he keeps a piece of seaweed in the garage which he consults daily.*

She woke up later that night when Evalina came in and felt guilty hearing sobs coming from the next bed.

Next morning she was awake first and quietly tore out a page from an exercise book. Taking a pencil she started to make a list to organise herself, as Bunny always did.

1.  Make sure who's collecting Jimmy.

2. What's for supper?
3. Try and write last line of "Streetwise"
4. Remember to tell Dad to get "Building Regulation permission" for loft
5. See Miss Thwaite first thing
6. Muffle up for the fog
7. Most important – find out about Penny Whistle
8. Read up geography homework

Evalina sat up in bed. 'What time is it? What are you doing?'

'I'm writing a list – I can't remember everything. Evalina, I'm really sorry about your things – your wig and...' she half expected another outburst. 'I honestly didn't mean...' But Evalina gave a big sigh.

'It didn't matter as things turned out. We waited over an hour for him to turn up and then, would you believe it, Mr Big himself turned out to be no more than a glorified messenger boy and it seems they just wanted a filing clerk at *New World*, no mention of modelling or photographs or anything like that! I was really glad I hadn't dolled myself up. I'd have felt a real fool.' She switched on her music. 'The awful thing is...' and she pulled a long face, 'I thought I was going to hand in my notice today and when I didn't get that rise, I wasn't exactly rude but I said some stupid things about not wanting to sit behind a desk anymore and what I thought of their new promotions idea and...'

'You asserted yourself,' said Alice remembering the word.

'You could say that. Anyway I've burnt my bridges

there and I liked the place really. I'll have to find a new job and start at the beginning again, and Mum will be worried.' She got out of bed listlessly. The alarm went off and Alice folded up her list. Evalina came and put an arm around her. 'Aren't you organised, making out lists?' She managed a small, wry smile. 'I suppose I'll have to start doing my own washing and ironing now with you so busy,' and for the first time, Alice decided it was nice to have a sister.

There was a note from Dad on the kitchen table. "Please feed cat. Warm milk and little water, money for shopping on hall chest."

Alice and the boys tended to the dog and the cat, who was due to go home that evening, and then started on their own breakfast while Evalina made herself some coffee – one teaspoon of powder, Alice noticed.

'What about supper tonight?' she asked, wondering if this was Amy's job.

'Don't bother about me – I'm going out,' Evalina said.

'How about your special chicken and sweet potato stew?' Danny asked. 'You haven't made it for ages – we'll help you with the vegetables.'

One meal was as difficult as another for Alice and at least they'd promised some help with this one.

'Well, write me a list of the things we usually put in and I'll do the shopping after school but you'll have to collect Jimmy tonight.' She would have to rush round the shops before meeting Thomas and she didn't yet know how long it would take her to find him.

Uncle Edgar put his head round the door. 'Well, I'm

off – I may be back later and maybe not.' He had an air of suppressed excitement about him but he didn't say any more as Chrissie arrived at that moment and there was a general rush to get ready for school, and settle the animals.

Alice didn't feel inclined to talk to Chrissie, who looked moody, so she concentrated her attention on Jimmy, holding his hand tightly as they crossed the busy road in the damp, grey atmosphere of the early morning: they couldn't keep up with Chrissie who had gone darting ahead.

Perhaps Jimmy might know something about the Penny Whistle – it was worth a try before asking at school or in the shops.

'Do you know Penny Whistle?' she asked and repeated "Penny Whistle".

Jimmy swung her hand backwards and forwards. 'Peter Piper Penny Whistle,' he chanted. It sounded like part of a nursery rhyme.

She tried again. 'Where is Penny Whistle?' But he just kept walking and swinging her hand and repeating 'Peter Piper, Penny Whistle,' so she gave up.

She had to report to Miss Thwaite before assembly and it took her a long time to find the staff room.

'Oh – there you are. I was wondering what had happened to you,' Miss Thwaite said briskly. 'I was very disappointed in your behaviour yesterday. We were all expecting great things from you and then you go and let yourself down like that. Whatever were you thinking of? Two centimetres of ribbon would have been ample and you took…'

Alice mumbled something about it being an accident.

'I believe your brother is doing very well at college,' Miss Thwaite brushed aside her explanation and gave her a penetrating look. 'You know you'll have to pull your socks up if you want to go into a profession and you'll have to work hard at the sciences.'

Without thinking Alice said, 'I want to be a hairdresser.'

Miss Thwaite drew back and her eyebrows shot up. 'I was told you had a serious ambition to do medicine!'

Alice was horror stuck – she'd let Amy down again. 'Well, I'll probably do that as well,' she said hastily.

'I don't like flippancy.'

A loud clanging bell brought the conversation to an end and Miss Thwaite dismissed Alice with a frown.

Luckily there was no science that day. By lunchtime, Dad's forecast had come true and a fog had descended leaving the school like a huge isolated island, drawing everyone inside closer together, as if to form a defence against the cold white sea swirling round outside. In the dining hall Alice started to ask casually about "Penny Whistle", going up to little groups and tossing the name in when she had an opportunity but she had no success.

'Alright what *is* Penny Whistle?'

Everyone thought it was the opening line of a joke 'Okay, tell us, what *is* the Penny Whistle, I give in.'

She saw Kev chatting to Chrissie but didn't go over to them. Kev waved at her and smiled, beckoning her to come over but she didn't want to tell Chrissie any of her plans. Although she might have solved the riddle of the

Penny Whistle, she would have thought it strange that Amy had had to ask.

During the afternoon, Alice found herself sitting next to a quiet red-haired boy, who was deeply engrossed in a boating magazine when he should have been concentrating on French conversation.

'I'll have that, Piper, *s'il vous plait*,' Mr Grice said wearily, putting his hand out.

Alice pricked up her ears at the name, remembering Jimmy's sing song, and leaned over to read the name on the exercise book lying on the next desk, as Piper handed over his magazine.

'And you can write me an essay on aspects of sea-sickness – *mal de mer* – using all irregular verbs. *Demain, s'il vous plait. Ca va?*'

The boy with the red hair groaned: Alice read "Nick Piper" on his book. Oh well, she hadn't really thought it would lead anywhere. At the end of the class she gathered her books together and looked out of the window – it was getting dark. She had the shopping to do and Dad had said 'go straight home.' Perhaps after she'd bought the vegetables she *would* go home.

'Amy, hey.' It look her a minute or two to react to her new name; she turned round to see Nick Piper talking to her. 'Message for Thomas from Pete. Could he give him a ring at the beginning of the holidays. At least I think that was what he said.'

'Pete – your brother?' Alice asked excitedly.

'Yes – Pete, my brother,' Nick said impatiently.

'The Penny Whistle,' Alice rushed on.

'What about it?'

He knew the "Penny Whistle'", he hadn't said, 'what are you talking about?'

'Where is it?' she asked quickly.

'Usual place of course – it's not likely to go anywhere is it?' He laughed sarcastically, collected his books and walked towards the door. Alice wondered desperately what she could say but Nick stopped and turned round, 'I was down by the canal the other week and they've given her a coat of paint – looks quite smart, *and* they're turning the old warehouse into a folk museum.'

'Yes, I've heard,' Alice lied.

Chrissie came up to her when school was over. 'Ready?' she asked curtly.

'I've got shopping to do – you go on without me.'

'Oh well, if you want to go on your own, suit yourself.' And Chrissie turned away sulkily leaving Alice to "muffle up" and find her way to the nearest shops in the darkening gloom.

There were colourful displays of vegetables at a brightly lit shop on the corner and some fruits which she couldn't recognise.

There was a deep freeze too and Alice picked out some chicken pieces, which were on the list of ingredients the boys had written down.

'Some ginger please and garlic and some coconut oil – and could you tell me the quickest way to the canal from here?'

The shop assistant collected the things up and then looked curiously at Alice 'What d'you want to go down to the canal for on an evening like this – I should go straight home if I were you.'

'It's my Dad – he's working on the old warehouse down there, they're turning it into a folk museum. I've got a message for him.' She surprised herself at the way she'd come out with the story.

Shaking his head in indignation and muttering, 'Well I wouldn't let a child of mine go wandering down there on their own…' he added up the amount of money she owed him and reluctantly gave her brief details of the best route to the warehouse by the lock.

Leaving behind the friendly lights of the shops, the street lamps and car headlights, Alice was plunged into the foggy gloom of side streets.

The houses there had a closed and secretive air about them, curtains drawn and doors firmly closed. One of these streets led down to a track by the side of the canal, which gleamed darkly and then shivered with fragments of light reflected from a single lamp, as a bird rustled among some reeds, disturbing the surface.

It was cold and desolate here and Alice huddled into her anorak. She wasn't sure what she was meant to be looking for; the sounds of the traffic were muffled now, but she kept imagining that she could hear footsteps following her, which stopped when she turned round. *Just the sound of the water lapping,* she told herself fiercely. She could just make out a huge black building looming up out of the mist on the left and saw that this part of the canal was congested with water craft of every sort and size. A large sign on the building said "Jepson's Wharf Warehouse, FOLK MUSEUM", with an announcement underneath saying "OPENING MARCH" and a final message underneath scrawled by an unknown hand read "SOME HOPE!!" There was no mention of Penny Whistle. She tried the door – it was locked. There were smaller, semi-derelict buildings nearby and an old boat repairs shop on the edge of the canal by a bridge. A lamp on the bridge threw a little light over the area and she crossed the tow path to see if the corrugated shed was open. Tied up alongside it was a barge, which, in spite of the disguise of a shiny coat of red paint, looked as it if had seen better days; cracked glass in the windows and rust spreading over the metal work gave this away. Along the side, decorated flamboyantly with swags of roses and leaves, was written the name, which immediately caught Alice's eye: "PENNY WHISTLE". She crept nearer to have a look. This must be where she was meant to meet Thomas. There was no sign of anyone. There was a narrow ledge under the windows of the boat and by edging her way gingerly along it she reached the small deck, then stood for a moment by the door to the cabin with its faded flower design. Moving forward, her foot caught in some frayed rope and she fell crashing forward, nearly pitching headlong into the dark interior as the door suddenly parted in the middle and slid back.

She saw a pair of startled eyes looking at her, then a large hand reached out and pulled her into the cabin. She guessed it was Thomas.

'You gave me a shock,' they said simultaneously.

'You're a bit late – thought you weren't coming.' She could see him more clearly now by the light of a flickering candle on a sturdy wooden table and he looked very like an older, worried version of Aldous.

Shabby dark curtains were drawn and although the doors were now closed, it seemed colder inside than out. The cabin was long and narrow; the floor looked damp and rotten and a dank musty smell hung in the air.

'I've been doing some shopping,' and Alice put the carrier bag down on the table. Thomas opened it up hopefully, took out a banana and ate it very quickly.

'I'm in some real trouble up to here,' he put a hand up to his neck, 'can't tell Dad, don't want to worry Mum, Evalina's hopeless, Edgar's pre-occupied, that leaves you.' And he pointed his finger at Alice then rummaged again in the bag for some more food.

'What can I do? Why are you here I thought...'

'I know, I know, everyone thinks I'm up at college, living in a flat in Seymour Street with a couple of friends and working hard and everyone's very proud.' He gave a half-mocking grin and huddled himself in his coat.

He certainly didn't look like the success story she'd imagined. She glanced round at the dingy surroundings and he saw the look.

'Well, it's a roof over my head and it's free. Peter's cousin said I could use it anytime – the key's always in the same place. Remember that party we had here when...' he pulled himself up sharply, 'anyway the fact is, I'm broke – haven't a penny – I had to borrow my fare down here. I blew the whole of my grant for the term in four weeks. Me, the financial wizard of the family, and I don't even know where it all went – just on taking friends out to meals, a few CDs, a few clothes. It just seemed to melt away. I'd never had so much money before in one lump sum.'

Alice thought she could understand his first term away from home and money in his pocket. She felt sorry for him. 'What are you going to do?'

'That's the big question. My tuition fees are paid already but I've no money to live on. I tried an evening job in a café but the hours were bad and I couldn't do that and concentrate on my work properly so I thought of something else – a moneylender – and that's been a real disaster. The loan kept me going for a couple of weeks but now I'm in debt with the interest rate charges. The whole thing's a terrible mess.' He put his head in his hands. 'I don't know what to do – I had to talk to someone.'

'What you need is a lot of money as soon as possible,' Alice was thinking aloud.

'I should have thought that was fairly obvious.' Thomas managed a wry smile.

'Like winning some money on a horse race or the football pools or premium bonds,' she went on.

'I don't have that sort of luck!'

'… or stocks and shares…'

'That's more my line – but what's the use. I've no hot tips for a quick profit and I've no money to invest. So we can forget that.'

But Alice had suddenly remembered something. The name "Nakavu" came to her mind. It was an unusual word and one which Bunny and Terry were constantly mentioning. A Japanese firm had designed a new micro disc, an improved product, more compact and with a mini wafer player at less price; their factory was to double its size and the firm was about to merge any day now with a similar company. Terry had heard about the secret merger talks going on through his contact with "Nakavu" and the discussions for plans for the enlargement, which he would be working on.

But it might be what Thomas had called a "hot tip" and she told him about it.

'Inside information – very interesting, "Nakavu" certainly sounds as if it's going places. I only wish I had some shares in it but I've nothing to invest – no money – remember?'

They both thought hard and at the same moment shouted 'The B Fund!'

'No, I couldn't,' Thomas said immediately and Alice shook her head.

'No, you couldn't really, could you?'

'It would only be borrowing if for a day or two.' Thomas considered for a moment. 'There's this guy at college – got credit with a stockbroker. He plays the market and a red hot tip like this!' He whistled expressively. 'I'll give him the money to show it's serious. That way, I'll make a profit on my investment *plus* a nice reward from him for the information. You *are* sure about all this, aren't you? Where did you hear about the merger?'

Alice nearly said 'From my father', but bit her lip and said quickly, 'Someone at school whose father's an architect. She said it was "top secret" and wouldn't tell anyone else.'

'Will you do it for me? Will you take it?'

Thomas looked at her pleadingly. He looked so thin – she was sure Mum and Dad would want to help him if they knew what had happened. They'd want to use their fund but it was still a risk. Thomas promised to have the money back intact in a few days, even if everything went wrong. 'I'll tell Mum and Dad everything and give up my place at college if I have to and take a job.'

There were papers and books spread over the table and Alice could see that he'd been trying to keep up with some of his work – well at least it was quiet here but so cold. She nodded her head, amazed at herself and the two of them left the freezing cabin.

He went with her through the streets back to Disraeli Drive and waited on the corner, leaning up against a lamp post while she turned into number six, opened the back door and put the shopping on the table.

She could hear Evalina singing up in their bedroom; the three boys sounded as if they were having a water pistol fight in the bathroom, Dad wasn't home yet and there was no sign of Uncle Edgar.

Tearing up some newspaper so that it looked the size of banknotes, she went into the sitting room.

The sick cat sat on a bright pink cushion by the fire and looked up at her accusingly as she reached up, standing on a chair, to the box containing the B Fund. She took all but the top two notes and some silver so as not to arouse suspicion immediately if someone just wanted a small amount. Then, substituting the newspaper to give bulk, she stretched the elastic band around the wad and slipped it back into the box. She put the chair back and was just putting the money into her pocket when she heard a voice behind her.

'What are you doing?' and turning round she saw

Chrissie's eyes, hard as black buttons, looking at her.

'Just tidying up a bit,' Alice said airily, her hand closing round the precious money in her pocket. She couldn't tell how long Chrissie had been standing there.

'My mum wants to borrow some sugar.'

'Help yourself.' Alice followed her into the kitchen. 'I've just got to pop out and post a letter.' She hurried out of the house to meet Thomas.

A bedroom window was opened and Evalina popped her head out. 'Hey! Where are you going? When are we having supper? I've got some news to tell you.'

'Just going to post a letter,' Alice shouted back. She couldn't stop. She raced to the corner of the road and Thomas' figure materialised out of the foggy night.

'You're a great girl, Amy,' he took the money. 'I'll return it on Friday. We'll just have to keep our fingers crossed that no-one misses it. I'll see you six o'clock – Penny Whistle,' he shouted and disappeared into the gloom.

Turning round to go home, Alice saw a shadowy figure dart away and heard running footsteps growing fainter.

Had they been overheard? She had the feeling that someone had been listening…

# SEVEN

Silently Amy had watched *Modern Art in the Ukraine* stealing a look now and then at Bunny and Terry who seemed absorbed in the programme. From time to time they would utter a cry of appreciation at a painting consisting of blobs of muted colour or a tortured looking piece of metal. A sculpture in sisal called "Seeds of Anarchy" brought a loud exclamation of praise from Bunny. 'It says everything doesn't it?' she turned to Amy who laughed and said, 'I must be going deaf.'

Bunny said sadly, 'I sometimes think you have no interpretative visual conceptions.'

When Amy laughed again at a pile of bricks entitled "Distress", Terry, breathing hard, turned off the television set and said softly to Bunny, 'I sometimes wonder why we try.' To Amy he said, 'Have you finished all your homework? You know your marks haven't been very promising lately – we'll have to have a word with Miss Lloyd at the parent/staff meeting on Thursday. Perhaps she can arrange for you to have some extra tuition.'

Amy thought that perhaps she was meant to be grateful for this suggestion, so said, 'Good idea, thanks.' But caught a look of surprise on his face.

Bunny consulted her watch. 'Do go and practice "Firefly", the Prescotts are coming round on Friday evening and you know how Amanda loves to hear your flute. They're bringing a couple who both work in television; he's written a book –*Wanderloom* – and she gives talks on Radio 3, they sound fascinating. Of course they're not coming till after "Quality Hour",' she added, as if to reassure Amy who looked blank.

Terry stood up. 'We must be off in a minute.'

Amy remembered them saying something about going to a private viewing of an art exhibition. She still felt hungry.

'Shall I make us all a big mug of cocoa and a slice of fruit cake before you go?' she offered, remembering the cake she'd seen Connie cutting into.

They both looked startled at the suggestion.

'Fruit cake, cocoa? I shouldn't think we have such things in the house – what are you thinking of?' Bunny almost shuddered.

'You still can't be hungry – you've only just had your supper.'

'But I only had…' Amy began.

Bunny laughed shortly. 'You don't imagine Connie's trying to starve you, do you? She knows you're a growing girl. It's just your age. Pop along now.'

Her timetable obviously said "flute practice" now, Amy thought.

'Goodnight then,' she said and gave Terry and Bunny a big hug as she did her own mum and dad at home. Alice's parents seemed unused to it.

It seemed to have taken Terry by surprise and nearly knocked him off balance – he had to clutch at a tubular white standard lamp to steady himself. Bunny too looked awkward and a little surprised at the sudden show of affection but then she gave a small shy smile, very like Alice's own, kissed her lightly on the head and said, 'Goodnight,' softly.

The bedroom was just as she'd left it, unlike her room shared with Evalina, where much of the time was spent trying to find things. Here, everything was in its place. The silence was a novelty and she sat down at the table to glance at the homework. It was a strange sensation being able to read undisturbed. Dimly, she was aware of the muffled bang of the front door as Bunny and Terry went out but read on until she started yawning.

Under the pillow on the bed, she found a pair of white and cream striped pyjamas. She wandered round the room while undressing, looking in drawers, tidy and lined with white paper, and the wardrobe where she spotted what must be the school uniform in cream and camel colours. She studied herself in the mirror again, running her hands over the smooth fair hair and wondered what the real Alice was like. A low, white bookshelf didn't reveal much of Alice's personality, it contained a set of handsome leather bound volumes of history of Europe; a present from her parents Amy saw, opening the front page of volume one and she thought they may have been chosen for their appearance rather than content.

By the bed was a small cupboard – the door was stiff as if the paint had stuck, but Amy pulled hard and it opened at last. Inside were two diaries – neither for this year – and both with clasps and locks, an assortment of holiday brochures for exotic far away places, and pages cut from fashion magazines. Looking through the cuttings, Amy saw that they were all photographs of hairstyles and some had been ringed with "Lucy's favourite" or "my favourite" written above them.

There were no keys to go with the diaries. Perhaps they were hidden away in a safe place and Amy wondered if Alice had kept a diary for this year, and who was Lucy?

She lay back on the bed and switched off the light. The silence was absolute and she drifted off to sleep peacefully, feeling as if she was floating away in clouds of cotton wool.

She didn't wake up until there was a sharp rap on her door the next morning and an equally sharp voice shouting, 'Half past seven.'

Amy couldn't think why everything was so quiet and the light switch was in a different place and then she remembered. It hadn't been a dream, she was still here in this pale, tranquil house and she was still "Alice Fraser". She stretched out, enjoying the peace and calm. No mad rush for the bathroom, no animals to feed, no family commitments as far as she could see – she felt she would enjoy the experience just for a day or two.

Her school uniform needed brightening up a bit – she'd see what she could find in the way of a ribbon or scarf.

Connie was downstairs, wearing a white overall, looking efficient but doing very little other than boiling water for the mint tea, which Terry and Bunny gulped down while standing around scanning the newspapers in silence. Amy sat at the table but was only offered some toast and marmalade. She was buttering her second piece when Terry looked at his watch. 'Come along Alice, what are you doing? You haven't fed Alabaster yet, have you?'

Who or what was Alabaster, Amy wondered. Connie unwittingly came to her aid.

'Your poor rabbit – I don't believe you even went near it yesterday evening, did you?'

A rabbit! It must be in the back garden. Amy opened the back door and found herself in the long back yard which she had glimpsed from the bathroom window. Much use of white paint, gravel and important looking urns and terracotta pots had transformed it into a strangely cold looking outdoor room complete with "all weather" white table and chairs. Instead of plants there were white painted branches and logs which had been carefully arranged around clusters of shiny pebbles and the focal point at the far end was a piece of modern sculpture: triangular, white and stark.

There was no place for a rabbit here but in an outhouse, perhaps once used for storing coal, Amy saw a wooden rabbit hutch containing a plump, white angora rabbit, which stared back at her through pink eyes.

'Alice,' she could hear Terry calling her and very quickly poured some "rabbit nuts", which she found in a sack nearby, into Alabaster's feeding bowl and refilled the water dish from a tap by the kitchen wall.

'I'll come and see you later,' she promised, then ran back into the house to find her coat and school books, on which were printed the words "Huxley House".

A short walk through the chilly, damp November morning brought them to some lock-up garages and then it was a tense drive through busy, commuter traffic to a huge pair of red brick houses built at the end of the 19th century, which had, added on to them at the side, a large modern extension. This was Huxley House, according to a large sign in the front gardens.

'Harriet's mother is bringing you home isn't she?' Terry said as she got out of the car.

'I think so,' Amy replied, cautiously.

'Well see if she can give you a lift tomorrow morning. We've got some big problem on The Retail Park at Harrington and I've got a working breakfast with the surveyors.'

Amy said, 'Goodbye,' but he hardly seemed to hear – he looked worried and preoccupied.

She looked around her then followed the others up a short drive bounded by a thick laurel hedge. Girls of all shapes and sizes, but all wearing "camel" coats, poured through an arched doorway.

'Oh well, here goes,' and Amy prepared to give herself up to the experience of Huxley House but just before she climbed the two steps to the open door, she was seized roughly by the arm by a large girl, who seemed to have sprung out from behind a damp rhododendron bush.

Amy pulled herself free. 'What's the matter?'

'What's the matter? Nothing's the matter, I hope. Where's that English essay you said you'd do for me? And we're having a spelling test today, so I hope you've done your homework.' The girl gripped her arm again menacingly. She was about to say something else when another girl called out, 'Come on Zell – we've got to report to Miss Nelson.' Zell gave Amy's arm a final painful twist, then released her and ran off.

If she had been her normal size, Amy would have been able to shake Zell's hand off with no trouble at all but, now that she was Alice, she felt weak and vulnerable.

'What was Zelda saying to you?' a girl her own height came up and linked arms with her and the two walked into school together.

'Something about an essay.' Amy wondered if it was the custom at Huxley House to work in pairs. If so, Zelda was going to be very disappointed – English was her worst subject.

'Look, I've got something to show you.' The other girl drew out of her coat pocket a piece torn from a magazine showing several hairstyles and colours. 'Which do you like best?' Amy pointed to a frothy creation in an unlikely shade of apricot pink.

'Yes, I like that one too.'

They had reached the cloakroom which smelt strongly of disinfectant and Amy's new friend stopped by one of the pegs and lockers.

Looking up quickly at the names above, Amy spotted "Alice Fraser" and "Lucy Braithwaite". It must be the Lucy marked on the cuttings in the bedside cupboard. She followed Lucy into a classroom smaller than those at her own school, with walls covered in prints of abstract paintings and large black and white photographs of world famous buildings.

The quiet buzz of conversation stopped and the whole class said, 'Good morning Miss Lloyd,' as a rather severe looking young woman came in carrying a load of books.

Amy sat down at a desk next to Lucy near the back and saw that she was also sitting next to Zelda.

The register was called and Amy remembered to say 'Yes' to her new name.

'Zelda Hulton-Price?'

'Yes, Miss Lloyd.'

The name, Hulton-Price, seemed vaguely familiar to Amy, although she couldn't think how or why. But there was no time to think about it as the class quickly and silently filed along the passage to the assembly hall and then afterwards back again to lessons. First, Geography and a test on the chief exports of South America, which luckily Amy had read up the previous night. Then French and a dictation and a test on "IR" verbs, which she couldn't do. And finally Maths, which consisted of a mental arithmetic test with questions fired at them in quick succession.

'Stop – you're going too fast!' Amy called out at one point. All heads swivelled round and looked at her in shocked surprise. She'd already startled the French class by her request to Monsieur Tati to read the dictation passages 'much more slowly.'

'That will do Alice. If you can't keep up leave a blank space.' And she was fixed with a glittering eye by the Maths master. She was pleased to get even ten marks out of fifty-five.

During a short break for fruit juice at eleven o'clock, she studied the notice board. A large section was given to lists of positions in class; weekly positions, showing marks, and monthly and term positions. Alice's name floated among the lower quarter. There were lists bearing brightly coloured stars by the sides of the names and a more sombre list with black stripes. Alice seemed to have gained no stars and two stripes, one for science and one for maths.

Her stomach was rumbling with hunger as they went into the hall for "Grecian Dancing and Free Expression".

'No, that won't do, Alice, your movements are a little too relaxed – we must all keep in strict tempo with the music – you're a wood nymph, remember, startled by something black and menacing lurking in the trees.' Mrs Tremble leapt forward in a deft movement to demonstrate, and signalled to the pianist to play the woodlands theme again.

'I don't think the nymph would be bothered by strict tempo if she was frightened – she'd run about like this,' and, to the other girls' amusement, Amy ran round the room giving a good impression of fear with much flinging around of her arms.

'When I need suggestions from you, I'll ask for them.' Mrs Tremble's voice was icy. 'You can sit out for the remainder of the lesson.'

Amy was glad to – she was feeling weak from hunger now and when the bell rang for lunch she couldn't help running down the corridor and pushing to the front of the queue forming by the dining hall where they'd had fruit juice at eleven o'clock. 'Come on Lucy,' she shouted.

'That will be two order marks, Alice Fraser,' a girl wearing a Prefect's badge bore down on her, 'one for running along the corridor and one for shouting and pushing. Tudor house is going to be very disappointed in you. Report to Miss Lloyd after lunch.'

Lunch was watery soup and some pale, unidentifiable fish, but there were plenty of vegetables and Amy helped herself to a huge portion. Lucy chattered away about a holiday abroad her sister was planning and when they'd finished their meal they were all expected to have "quiet reading" with a book in the library.

'That's three order marks in one morning,' Miss Lloyd exploded. 'How did you come to miss your flute lesson? Poor Mr Varley sat there for half an hour waiting for you.'

'I left my flute at home.' Amy felt sorry for the mess she was getting Alice into.

'... And I've had complaints from Monsieur Tati and Mrs Tremble about your rudeness in class.'

'I wasn't rude –' Amy began but Miss Lloyd cut her short.

'Don't make matters worse. This isn't going to look good on your report and I shall have to say something to your father at the parent/staff meeting on Thursday. I don't know what's come over you. Now go and get ready for your biology or you're going to miss that.'

Biology! Her best subject.

'Open your books at page 105. We'll continue with the amoeba,' Mrs Fry started enthusiastically.

Amy couldn't stop herself, 'Oh – but I've done the amoeba already – I've finished it and the hydra.'

There was a horrible silence and then someone gave a nervous laugh. Mrs Fry looked as if she couldn't believe her ears.

'You've done the amoeba already! You consider your knowledge of the amoeba is completely adequate, do you? Well, could you kindly explain why you came bottom of the class on the test we had last week?'

Amy bit her lip and said nothing while others, including Mrs Fry, laughed now.

'Perhaps you'd like to come and take the lesson – here's the chalk.' Mrs Fry held out the piece of chalk with mock solemnity and turned to the rest of the class while waiting for "Alice" to apologise, but Amy took up the chalk, strode over to the blackboard and drew a picture of the amoeba and the hydra, naming all the parts.

Strangely, Mrs Fry didn't seem very pleased. She snatched back her piece of chalk muttering something about 'exhibitionist' and ignored Amy for the rest of the lesson. It had been a disaster and she had hoped to get a star for Alice.

Lucy nudged her. 'Are you trying to get yourself expelled or something?'

The lesson called "Three Dimensional Ceramics" turned out to be pottery and was more enjoyable. Amy became absorbed in modelling a sugar bowl out of clay, which looked like a hat upside down.

The studio was also used for painting and dressmaking, and Amy spied some pieces of bright fabric in a waste paper basket which she slipped into her pocket.

'Have you learnt your spelling?' Lucy whispered when they were back in their classroom.

'No talking.' Miss Lloyd shuffled some papers. Zelda moved her desk slightly nearer to Amy's and Lucy was told to distribute a piece of blank paper to everyone.

'Names on the top as usual. Are we ready?' There was a moment of tense silence, then Miss Lloyd rattled off a list of words like rhythm, accessible, vicious and perennial, at such speed that Amy didn't even have time to object.

Spelling was another of her least favourite subjects and she was surprised to see Zelda glancing at her piece of paper and then write quickly on her own. *She won't have much luck if she's trying to copy mine,* she thought.

A complicated method of marking each other's efforts followed and Amy and Zelda tied for bottom place, which brought more sarcasm and annoyance from Miss Lloyd and some extra homework.

The bell rang and it was time for home. Amy, without knowing why, felt somehow that her day at Huxley House had not been a great success. She gathered up her books and went to put on her coat, while Lucy made plans to ask her to tea next week before rushing off. She had already spotted Harriet, whose mother was to give her a lift home, and was just about to follow her out of the door when she felt a cold hand clutch her round the back of the neck.

'You did that on purpose, didn't you?' Zelda, looking furious, dragged her into a lobby full of hockey sticks and slammed the door.

'All that spelling – all those words – you wrote the whole lot wrong on purpose just to get me into trouble!' she screamed.

'You didn't have to copy mine,' Amy replied, coolly.

'Ha Ha! Very funny!' But she didn't look amused. 'I think you've forgotten our little agreement, haven't you?' She pushed her face near to Amy's, scowling, until Amy could have counted her pale eyelashes and freckles.

'You'd better not forget, Alice Lettice Fraser, that I've got your diary and I've read every word – all you've put in about "Lippy" Lloyd and "Ratty" Tati and I'm going to take it straight to Miss Lloyd tomorrow if you don't swear to keep your part of the bargain. I want good marks in spelling tomorrow and that essay – do you understand!' She took Amy by the shoulders, shook her, and then shoved her into the pile of hockey sticks.

Amy sat there for a minute trying to work things out. Alice was being blackmailed – she must have taken her diary to school one day and, unluckily for her, it had been read and stolen by Zelda Hulton-Price and she was too frightened to mention it to anyone as she'd written some rude comments about the staff. She must be good at English and spelling and so Zelda was able to take advantage of this and bully Alice into giving her all the help she wanted. Zelda Hulton-Price... Hulton-Price. She still couldn't remember where she'd heard that name.

She must find Harriet or they might go off without her!

Harriet's mother, whom everyone, including Harriet, called "Jinty" was tapping her fingers impatiently on the driving wheel of her car as Amy and Harriet squeezed in with three other girls and Harriet's two younger brothers.

The journey home was rowdy and reminded Amy, with a pang, of her own family – the noise and the jokes, but she pushed those thoughts to the back of her mind – *I'll be back with them soon.* She was looking forward again to being inside the pale, quiet house in Rosetti Grove with no demands being made of her.

She was ravenously hungry again and, after asking "Jinty" if she could take her to school the next morning, she ran up to the door of number eleven, fantasising about a large plate of ham and tomato sandwiches with lots of mayonnaise, a big pot of tea, made the way Mum and Dad liked and a huge hunk of that fruit cake she'd seen last night.

The door was opened by Connie who greeted her without enthusiasm.

'Slippers on – start your homework and your tea will be ready at five o'clock,' she said.

Amy had forgotten the strict timetable kept at Rosetti Grove.

'Can I have a piece of fruit cake and a glass of milk to take up with me – I'm starving,' she said.

'What fruit cake?' Connie went into the kitchen and closed the door behind her.

The silence in the house was almost tangible, broken only by rumblings of Amy's stomach as she moved silently up the stairs to the bathroom to wash her hands.

Out of the window, she could see into the garden next door and it looked more like her own garden back at home in Disraeli Drive: a patchy lawn, a small vegetable plot and under a leafless old apple tree, long grass and weeds. It was starting to get dark.

She remembered the rabbit, Alabaster – he'd love some dandelion leaves.

Connie was going upstairs to her room – she could hear the soft pad, pad of her footsteps going past the bathroom door.

She raced down the stairs two at a time and went into the kitchen. The white paint everywhere caused the room to glow strangely in the twilight. There was not an item out of place; the floor looked like a mirror.

*I wonder where she hid that cake, she can't have eaten it all and I wonder why she pretended there wasn't any?* Amy thought and started opening the shiny cupboards and smoothly running fitted units. There was very little in any of them. A white metal vegetable rack held a small tin of peas and the large bread bin contained half a sliced loaf and a packet of rye bread.

Inside the giant refrigerator were only two bottles of skimmed milk, some margarine, six eggs, a bottle of mineral water and an avocado pear. Just enough for the light supper on a tray upstairs she'd heard Bunny mention that morning.

The stainless steel stove looked impressive and complicated, with knobs and switches and many dials. She was sure it would hold an enormous turkey at Christmas but couldn't imagine it ever being used for that purpose in this household. She opened it up and a light went on, illuminating, to Amy's surprise, a large store of tins and packets, plus the remains of the fruit cake.

Sitting back on her heels, she took out a few of the tins: smoked oysters, chicken breasts, anchovy fillets, black cherries. Her mouth started watering – they were not everyday items of food but expensive luxuries. *Well at least I can cut myself a slice of cake,* she thought. She didn't hear the door open softly as she stood up to find a knife.

'May I ask what you're doing?'

# EIGHT

Amy swung round and found Connie in the doorway looking furious.

'I was looking for something to eat.'

'Well, you won't find it there.' Connie bundled back the tins quickly and slammed the oven door. 'Those are emergency rations and not to be touched.'

Alice might have been satisfied by that explanation, Amy thought, but she wasn't convinced and faced Connie's cold stare defiantly, before going out to see to Alabaster.

She could hear boxes being moved about in the garden next door and, standing on a large piece of granite which had been carefully placed in the centre of a small area of gravel near the fence, she peered over.

The boy she'd seen from the upstairs window was heaving empty tea chests into a small outhouse.

'Hello,' she called, 'I was wondering if I could have some of those leaves for my rabbit. There's nothing in the garden here only stones and pebbles and pots.'

'Do you live there?' He looked up at Amy and for a moment she nearly said 'No, of course not.' And then remembered that she was Alice.

His name was Sam – they'd just moved in and he was going to Parkwood High School. He had a younger brother and a couple of stick insects.

He pulled up some leaves in the gathering dusk, handed them over the wall and said he'd like to come round and see Alabaster some time. Then a voice called 'Sam!' from inside his house and he vanished.

She spent a moment or two with the rabbit then Connie shouted 'Tea' very curtly and Amy went back inside. She was so hungry by now that she had started to look enviously at Alabaster nibbling his greenery.

Connie was silent as she poured a cup of weak tea from a stainless steel teapot. On a white plate were two slices of bread and butter, placed each side of a boiled egg.

'You'd better hurry up and eat your tea – you haven't started your homework yet, have you? You're behind schedule.'

Amy wondered what was on the timetable for this evening. She was still puzzled by the food in the oven and Connie seemed to guess her thoughts.

'Those tins you saw – I bought them from a sale at Lenco's the other day – discontinued lines – quite a saving,' she said in a flat voice. Amy said nothing but somehow didn't believe her.

Tea was finished in three minutes; she took her dishes to the machine in the corner and then escaped up the stairs, nearly knocking into Terry who was going at a slower pace carrying a huge flat board like an enormous tray, on which lay a number of blocks of varying size.

'Steady, steady,' he sounded agitated. 'You nearly destroyed months of hard work.'

Bunny came up the stairs behind them.

'It's the model for the Retail Park,' she said in hushed almost reverential tones. Then her voice changed, became more brisk. 'Shouldn't you be practicing your flute?' She looked at her watch. 'We may have to put Q.H. back a little – we'll be busy working on this,' She waved a hand towards the model, 'but Terry's promised you a game of monopoly and we won't let you down.'

Inside her quiet room, Amy had time to think. *What was "Q.H." which had to be put back?* Then she remembered Bunny saying something about some friends of theirs coming on Friday evening after 'Quality Hour' – it would be interesting to see what the quality consisted of – she was sure it would last exactly sixty minutes. Amy felt she was just as busy here, though in a quiet intense way, as she was at home.

Well, not knowing where the flute was kept, she couldn't even blow a few notes. She'd try to concentrate on some homework and not let Alice down on the spelling again.

While she sorted out her books, her mind wandered back to the food in the oven. Were Bunny and Terry aware of its existence? She remembered Connie's brother leaving hastily with his carrier bag. Did Connie feed him when he came here – did the two of them feast themselves at Bunny and Terry's expense while Alice almost starved?

It was easy to work here with no Evalina bustling about the bedroom and no boys bursting in, shouting or quarrelling; no Uncle Edgar with his music or Aunt Seely arriving uninvited.

The door of the bedroom opened and Terry popped his head round. He looked hurt.

'It's quarter to seven. I've been waiting for you with the Monopoly board set out. It's bad of you to keep us waiting, especially as we're so busy at the moment.'

Amy leapt up. 'Sorry,' she said.

Down in the sitting room, the fake log fire had been switched on and in front of it, on a cream coloured coffee table, the game had been carefully arranged. Two spiky grey stools were pulled up to it while on an equally uncomfortable looking armchair Bunny sat, looking at her watch reproachfully. A C.D. of Chopin's Preludes was playing softly.

'I'll take the top hat, which do you want?' Terry asked, picking out the counters from the box where the money and property cards were neatly displayed.

Amy only half remembered Monopoly. Thomas had had a set once but Danny and Aldous had rifled the box and used the money for a game of their own. She knew the main thing was to acquire property and put up houses and hotels, collecting rent from those.

'The car, please,' she said, and settled down to concentrate. She bought speedily and recklessly anything on which the car landed, mortgaged streets and put up hotels while Terry was in "jail" and in thirty minutes he was bankrupt. He looked surprised and weary as he put his hand to his forehead.

'Afraid I wasn't concentrating this evening – rather a lot on my mind.'

Bunny had been watching the game. 'You're usually so cautious,' she said critically.

'Just on a lucky winning streak.' Amy smiled and started to tidy up.

'Come and enjoy the Chopin quietly for a few minutes. These preludes are arranged in order of each major key, followed by one in its relative minor, which is unusual, isn't it?'

'Whatever,' Amy muttered.

They all listened to the piano music for a few minutes. Then Bunny produced some postcards she'd bought at the Northend Galleries where they'd attended the private viewing of an art exhibition the previous evening.

Each card was discussed and analysed.

'I particularly like this one – "Sigh on The Wind",' Bunny said holding up one which was blank apart from an almost colourless beige streak. 'What do you think?'

'Spilt tea?' Amy asked.

Bunny sighed and selected another card.

'Can you see the symbolism in this? It's called "Evidence".' Pale blue background surrounded by a splodge of orangey-brown, with steamy swirls of smoky grey rising up from it. 'It's so clever,' Bunny enthused. 'You can see the truth – the central truth of the matter.'

Amy thought, *What on earth is she going on about?* She said, 'Evidence of dog sick, or worse, on pale blue carpet, if you ask me!'

Terry's usual pale face was flushed, his cheeks puffed out and Amy felt he looked as if he might explode but he managed to control himself and his voice just sounded sorrowful.

'Shall we show Alice our big surprise or leave it until she's feeling a little more mature?'

Bunny considered. 'I really want to see it again myself. I can't help thinking we probably paid too much for it... but you know,' she said turning to Amy, 'it just spoke to us.'

*This sounds far more interesting,* Amy thought... *Perhaps it's a parrot.*

Terry went over to a corner of the room and picked up something square-shaped, shrouded by a beige and grey shawl.

'Right, you can perform the unveiling ceremony,' he told Amy, as if conferring on her a great honour.

She jumped up and pulled back the shawl to reveal a stark oil painting in black and white. It resembled nothing that Amy could recognise – the shapes and blobs forming an irregular circle in the centre, surrounded by squiggles, which looked as if they had been applied by a trowel.

She drew back, thinking how hideous it was.

'What does it say to you?' Bunny was looking at the picture but speaking to Amy. 'It's called "Repression".'

'I'm not surprised,' Amy muttered.

'You feel it too?' Bunny was delighted. 'To me, it explores new concepts of poetic dimension; it says... Quell, crush... Of course, it could be taken as a celebration of humility, don't you think? I can see a face with half closed eyes.' They all peered closely at the canvas.

'That looks like a giraffe.' Amy pointed to a cluster of spots with a thick splodge of black paint rising up from it.

'No, I don't think so,' Bunny said uncertainly.

'Perfect balance and symmetry,' murmured Terry. A picture hook had already been fixed on to the wall and "Repression" was now hung ceremoniously.

There was a sound at the door: Terry looked at his watch as Connie entered the room carrying a tray of poached eggs, avocado pear and two glasses of mineral water; she avoided Amy's eyes. When she left the room, Amy said, 'Connie keeps food in the oven.'

'And what better place for it,' Terry said reaching for his poached egg on toast. Bunny, sipping her mineral water, was still admiring the painting.

'Time you went and finished your homework. We're going to the parent/staff meeting at your school tomorrow – hope Miss Lloyd will have some nice things to say about you.'

Amy thought back over the day. It hadn't gone well. She had let Alice down and there was that business about Zelda and the diary.

She sat down again. 'I don't know whether she will – things haven't been going so well and there's this girl…' She would have told everything to Mum and Dad at her own home and together they would have sorted things out, but Terry just said, 'Well, we'll talk about it tomorrow with Miss Lloyd.' She kissed them goodnight and went up to the bedroom. It seemed an odd idea to her to have an appointment system with your own parents.

Later, there was a wheaty flake and some skimmed milk on the kitchen table for her supper, which she ate while Connie, not saying a word, made heavy weather over cleaning out a drawer.

After her bath, Amy took out the new toothbrush, which she had found last night with three others, still in their wrappers, in a small cupboard. She didn't like the flavour of the toothpaste which Alice used, preferring her own tube of "Frudent" – strawberry flavour, which Evalina bought at discount price from the factory where she worked.

Evalina and the Frudent factory – they seemed a million miles away! But, suddenly, Amy remembered something which made them seem much nearer. Something to do with Zelda Hulton-Price and she smiled as big a smile as she could manage on Alice's face.

Harriet's mother was late with the school run next morning. Amy had had time, after rushing her inadequate breakfast, to make an impromptu wide and colourful hair band from the pieces of material she'd found in the art room. She was pleased with the result and slipped it over her hair in the car – it would add a much needed touch of colour to the insipid school uniform.

'You'll never get away with it,' Harriet said.

Before she'd reached her classroom, she was the object of stares and nudges.

Miss Lloyd pounced. 'Alice Fraser – whatever do you think that is on your head? You look like a... a... ' her imagination failed her. 'Take it off at once. You know you're not allowed to wear anything of the sort!'

'It's only a hair band – to keep my hair tidy,' Amy explained, 'and brighten things up a bit.'

'Don't answer back! That will be two stripes – and your parents coming to the meeting tonight, they're going to be very, very disappointed.'

Lucy gave Amy a sympathetic look while Zelda was smiling into her open desk.

That morning there was History, with dates being chanted out loud, Singing, Art Appreciation and French, where she crossed swords once more with Monsieur Tati.

After lunch, Zelda caught up with her in the corridor and manoeuvred her into a small room, not much larger than a cupboard, where brushes, mops and buckets were kept.

'Where is it then? Come on – the essay!' She loomed threateningly over Amy.

'I haven't done it and I'm not going to!'

A look of disbelief passed over Zelda's face, followed by one of anger.

'… And I'd like my diary back, please.'

'Your diary back!' Zelda mocked. 'It's going straight to Miss Lloyd unless you sit down now and write that essay for me.'

Amy lounged back against the wall and smiled.

'Did your father ever work at the toothpaste factory? "Frudent"?'

The question caught Zelda unawares, she looked startled. 'Well what if he did?'

'I know someone who works there. She told me a very funny story of one of the scientists who was working on the fruit flavours. Well, he got the formula all wrong and they came out tasting of sardines! I think he had to leave. All the tubes of toothpaste had to be destroyed. Can you imagine cleaning your teeth with sardines!' she laughed.

The freckles on Zelda's face vanished into the bright flush which had spread over her face. Her expression changed to one of fear and then pleading.

'Don't tell anyone, will you – promise? I'll give you your diary; I won't show it to a soul, honestly. Promise you won't tell?'

Evalina's factory gossip had been useful and Amy was glad she'd remembered Harry Hulton-Price and the fishy flavour.

'I'll see.' Amy couldn't help prolonging the agony a bit. 'Everyone will enjoy the story. It'll make a good laugh. Sardines! I can see it now. We can all make fish faces – great!' She rolled her eyes and pursed her lips together, opening and closing them quickly in a good imitation. 'Oh yes!'

Tears of rage and frustration were now running down Zelda's cheeks. She leant back against the door looking tired and defeated. The door suddenly swung open and she staggered into Miss Lloyd.

'I thought I heard voices in here. You should be getting ready for netball – you know you're not allowed...' She broke off seeing Zelda's distressed state.

'What's the matter?' She saw Amy, 'Alice Fraser – so it's bullying now, is it? You should...'

She felt it had been on the tip of Miss Lloyd's tongue to say 'You should pick on someone your own size', but had then realised that Zelda was by far the taller of the two.

Zelda began to say 'It's not really…' but Miss Lloyd chipped in. 'I appreciate that you don't wish to tell tales, Zelda, but I think I am a good judge of a situation. This will mean a detention Alice and, of course, I shall have to tell Mrs Winterbourne. She ushered them out of the room. 'Amy you'd better move desks so that you don't sit near each other. Come along Zelda.' And she walked away down the corridor as the bell rang.

The others did indoor netball practice while Amy sat with a pile of extra work, looking out of the window at the fog from time to time.

The silence in the classroom seemed oppressive now. She stared at the books in front of her. *I don't have to do all this work,* she thought. *I can just wish myself back if I want and leave it all.* But she then felt guilty at all the trouble she'd unwittingly caused which Alice would have to sort out. I'll stay a bit longer, she decided.

Zelda had moved into a desk at the opposite side of the classroom and Amy was now sitting next to Harriet on one side.

'Good idea of yours about the hairbands – we've been talking about it,' Harriet said after netball practice, as Amy moved her books into her new desk. 'We're going to set up a petition for them, and coloured ribbons and hair slides, instead of the old brown ones. I don't see why we shouldn't have a bit of colour. I'd like bright green!' She brought out a piece of paper. 'I've just written this: We, the undersigned, would like to have the opportunity of expressing our personalities in the form of our own choice of head apparel in place of the uniform brown ribbons and slides.'

'You can sign at the top – it was your idea in the first place.'

Amy wrote "Alice Fraser". Then Harriet took it round for another to sign.

Mrs Winterbourne, the Head, took the final lesson of the day – English Literature. She admired Shakespeare above all other writers and her classes were always made to learn chunks of *Hamlet* or *Macbeth* – regardless of whether they understood the whole story or not.

The last piece set had been from *Julius Caesar* and Mrs Winterbourne pounced on members of the class at random. "Friends, Romans and Countrymen" droned on uninspired and hesitatingly, or briskly and without comprehension.

'Alice.'

Amy stood up. She hadn't learnt the piece, she didn't know any Shakespeare but she remembered the poem she had had to learn last week.

'I don't know it… but I can say "The Buttercup",' and she launched into a short modern piece comparing a buttercup to a fried egg.

Some stifled giggles were quelled by a look from Mrs Winterbourne.

'What nonsense is this – what sort of exchange is this for "the Bard"?' How dare you decide what you shall or shall not learn? Such insolence!' She shook her head sadly and gave Amy extra speeches to learn.

Harriet handed in her petition at the end of the lesson

but Mrs Winterbourne swept it up with her papers without looking at it.

The journey home was slow because of the fog.

Bunny opened the door. 'Connie's half day off – you'll have to get your own tea today. We'll have a piece of brie and a tomato when we get back from your school. We really shouldn't be going out anywhere this evening. We're busy wrestling with this circulation problem – we don't seem to be getting anywhere – very worrying.' She disappeared upstairs.

So, it was Connie's evening off! Well, she'd make sure she'd have a proper tea and she'd cook a feast of a supper for the three of them, Amy decided. She'd raid the emergency stores and cook up something tasty and filling. Bunny and Terry looked as if they could use a square meal.

A large pot of tea, scrambled egg on toast with grilled tomatoes and then more toast and the rest of the pot of jam took the edge off her appetite. She discovered a small white radio on the window sill, half hidden by an arrangement of dead twigs in a slender glass vase and by twiddling the knobs, found some cheerful music – she was beginning to dislike the perpetual unearthly silence.

Alabaster was brought into the kitchen to stretch his legs and hopped about under the table, his strange pink eyes expressionless at his new found freedom.

'A longer run next time,' Amy promised, lifting him back into his hutch.

In the gloom of the back garden she heard a window open in the house next door and could just make out the silhouette of Sam's head against the light.

'Busy at the moment – I'll come round and see your rabbit on Friday.' The sash window banged down and he was gone.

Amy could hear the telephone ringing in the hall and no one seemed to be answering it. She picked up the receiver.

'This is Coopers' Delicatessen and Groceries.' After checking it was the Fraser household, the voice at the other end said a few brusque words, something about a second reminder, a Friday deadline and he'd be obliged, all of which made little sense to Amy. She tried to repeat the message to Bunny and Terry before they set off for Huxley House but Bunny shook her head vaguely. 'Can't think what he's talking about. Connie sees to all that side of things, she'll sort it out. Now. Mrs Hayday is up in the sitting room and she'll stay until we get back. You get on with your homework and music practice – we should be back at eight o'clock.' A quick look at their watches and they were gone.

Amy sighed. She didn't think that she'd done anything wrong at school; she hadn't lied, stolen or cheated. Perhaps it would be alright. 'It'll be alright on the night,' she remembered hearing from somewhere and chanted it to herself.

At half past seven it was time to start preparing the meal. Amy planned to create something delicious – she enjoyed experimenting and the food she'd seen in the oven fired her imagination. The light went on as she opened the oven door but instead of the tins and packets she'd seen previously, an empty space was revealed. There was nothing there – it was completely empty.

A quick look in the cupboards and drawers didn't solve the mystery. Bunny and Terry seemed disinterested in food so that left Connie – she had taken "the rations" somewhere, stolen them.

She found some flour and a piece of cheese in the fridge. *A cheese soufflé,* she thought, *and then pancakes.* While she grated the cheese and whisked the eggs, she wondered how she could bring the situation to Bunny and Terry's attention. It seemed all wrong that Alice was being half starved while at the same time good food was passing through the house. Connie was in sole charge of domestic arrangements while Alice's parents were busily pre-occupied with their work.

The soufflé rose but fell again as the minutes ticked by.

Eventually, Amy heard the front door open. Mrs Hayday departed and Bunny and Terry came to find her. They looked both weary and cross, and sank down on to the uncomfortable kitchen stools. The fog had been bad. Their timetable had been seriously disrupted and, by the look on their faces, Amy gathered they hadn't heard what they'd hoped to hear at the school meeting.

'I've made a cheese soufflé but it's sunk… and all the rations from the oven have gone.'

Bunny looked bewildered and Terry said, 'Never mind all this talk of food – if you gave as much concentration to your work at school it might be a better thing.' He sought to restore himself with a glass of mineral water.

Bunny still looked dazed. 'I still can't quite believe it – when Miss Lloyd was saying all those things, it just didn't sound like you. I even said to her "Surely you must be making a mistake – Alice isn't like that".'

Amy sat down on a stool. 'What did she say?'

'Well, it wasn't only Miss Lloyd... Monsieur Tati was quite unpleasant, he mentioned insubordination.'

'Mr Varley said you missed a flute lesson,' Terry took up the tale of woe, 'Mrs Fry said you were showing off in the biology lesson – you've had stripes and order marks – breaking rules and flouting authority and today, worst of all, Miss Lloyd apparently found you intimidating one of the other girls.'

'It isn't like that – you don't understand.' Amy didn't know how to begin explaining.

'Mrs Winterbourne is very worried – we don't know what to make of it all – Huxley House was recommended to us by the Prescotts,' Bunny said. 'I'm beginning to wonder if the place is having a bad influence on you.'

Amy put on the black oven gloves and lifted the hot cheese dish out of the oven.

'I think we may have to consider removing you from the school,' and Terry gazed bleakly at the sagging soufflé, 'they say you're too assertive.'

*Oh no!* Amy's heart sank as she automatically dished out the meal. *Whatever will Alice think – what have I done? I've really landed her in a heap of trouble.*

# NINE

Alice had worried about Thomas and the money for the rest of the week. In between school, shopping, looking after Jimmy and assorted animals, she wondered how long it would be before the loss of the B Fund was discovered.

Luckily there was no more science that week and she was able to cope with most other subjects, although it was nearly impossible to find the time and peace to do any homework.

Uncle Edgar appeared to have vanished off the face of the earth but the others didn't seem unduly worried – he was apparently in the habit of going away for short periods to stay with friends, play music, appear in a few clubs with his group called "Sugar Beat" and then reappear in the caravan without warning. Aunt Seely disapproved of all this and said so constantly, while dropping in for a meal which Alice conjured up using all sorts of interesting bits and pieces. The chicken and sweet potato stew had turned out well and she was now enjoying experimenting with food and inventing new recipes.

Over a steaming hot curry on Thursday evening, Dad said, 'We're in for a wet weekend, squalls and cloud bursts, but all being well, there's one bright spot – Mum should be coming home on Sunday afternoon. We'll have to have a party.'

'Chocolate cake!' Jimmy shouted looking at Alice but she had decided that by Sunday she should be back in Rosetti Grove. Amy should be here among her family to welcome Mum home while *she* was beginning to look forward to some peace and quiet and time to think.

Evalina had been to see Mum in hospital and had told her the good news of her new job; still at "Frudent", but one of the management had been impressed with her ideas and criticism when she'd asked for a rise and had offered her a position in marketing and sales promotions. 'I'm really excited about it – and I may get a small rise in salary too.'

'Toothpaste with a bite – it's blackberry white,' she sang, 'our new flavour – blackberry.'

Donny and Aldous started to yawn with mock boredom. 'Tell us about the new room again, Dad,' Aldous said. The idea of a den in the loft appealed to them.

'Well, *you* won't be allowed in it,' Dad teased. 'It's going to be a place of peace and quiet, absolutely no noise, a sanctum – Amy's idea. I think the extension should work quite well. I've been in touch with the planning authorities and there seem to be no problems there. Mum and I have been discussing it and we've decided to use the 'B' fund to pay for it. I've even had a word with that friend of Edgar's, Bob Pope – we could start quite soon.'

'Not the B Fund,' Danny groaned and everyone looked miserable, 'that's for your FANTASTIC holiday – you and Mum – Barbados.'

'I know, I know, but there's plenty of time for that – we can start saving again. This is more urgent. How much is in the fund? Go and fetch the box.'

Alice went through to the sitting room feeling weak and trembling. What could she do? She'd promised not to tell anyone. She reached up for the box, wondering if, by some miracle, Thomas had somehow managed to slip the money back in again, but a quick look showed her that he hadn't.

Dad took the box and opened it, reading the amount on the piece of paper on top.

'That's a lot of money saved up.'

It didn't seem as if he was going to bother counting it. He closed the lid. Alice held her breath.

Then Chrissie, who'd joined them with her mother for the curry supper, looked sly and said, 'Why don't you count it, to make sure.' She bent her head, with a brilliantly coloured butterfly slide in her hair, over the box and watched while Dad smiled and said, 'Why not?'

Aunt Seely let out an unpleasant noise – a cross between a squawk and a croak when they saw all the money had gone. The shock and horror made Jimmy start to wail, without quite understanding what all the fuss was about.

'Where's Edgar gone – that's what I'd like to know,' Aunt Seely nodded sagely.

'Now Cecilie.' Dad used her full name, he looked grave. 'You can't go accusing anyone.'But Aunt Seely went on nodding.

*This is terrible,* Alice thought, *they're going to think Uncle Edgar's taken it.*

Chrissie's head suddenly swivelled round and she looked at Alice with spiteful eyes. 'Perhaps Amy knows something about it.'

Everyone looked at Amy.

'Why should she?' Dad asked.

Chrissie shrugged but went on staring at her.

They were all waiting for her to say something. What would Amy have said?

'I do know something about it but I can't say any more until tomorrow night.' Alice heard herself speak in a low soft voice. 'It'll be alright, really.'

But she felt everyone's hostility and disgust.

'I can't believe that you took the money.' Dad looked sad and disappointed.

'It will be alright,' she repeated, hoping that it really would be. She had had no access to the financial columns of any newspapers. When the *Reminder* arrived early, Dad took it to work.

'I trust you – but tomorrow…' Dad looked worn out.

'Well, I think you're mad.' Aunt Seely shook her head, hauled herself out of her chair and grabbed Chrissie, who was smiling a secret smile.

'I'm not asking for your opinion,' Dad said and opened the door for her.

The boys were subdued for once and went up quietly to their room without a glance at Alice.

Dad put the box back and went to have a look at a neighbour's small cross-bred dog which had a limp.

'Cheer up,' Evalina tweaked Alice's hair. 'It'll come out in the wash.' Then she grinned wryly, remembering the disaster at the launderette, 'but not like my wig, I hope.' She was going out with Paul so Alice was left on her own. Jimmy didn't ask her for a story and she heard Aldous reading to him.

She went to bed early but couldn't sleep.

Chrissie didn't call for her the next morning, after a breakfast which was unusually quiet. Alice took Jimmy to play school through wet, windy streets and spent the morning feeling nervous and worried, unable to concentrate on her History project or woodwork. She caught sight of Chrissie and Kev at lunchtime and thought he turned to look the other way – what had Chrissie been telling him?

The afternoon seemed to drag but at last school was over for the day and, grabbing her anorak, Alice rushed out of the main entrance.

'Hang on, hang on.' A voice called her back. 'Are you that eager to leave us, Amy?' It was Mr Cox, the English master. She stood on one foot, impatient to be off.

'It's been decided by the powers that be, that the production next term will be the "Insect Play" and I think there'll be a part in it for you – one of the moths perhaps. How would you like that?'

'That's great.' Alice hoped that Amy would be pleased.

Mr Cox started to tell the story of the play – his ginger hair blowing in the wind, his face lit by enthusiasm.

Alice shifted to her other foot. It was freezing standing there, although Mr Cox didn't seem to notice the cold, despite his nose turning pink.

'Are you impatient to be off?'

'It's not that but I've got shopping to do. The play sounds wonderful.' Half of her wished she could really take part in it.

'Off you go then.'

She ran down the drive, overtaking groups who were loitering and chatting together before going home. It was true that she had some shopping to do and it was too early to meet Thomas yet – he'd said six o'clock.

Already it was getting dark and she was glad to join some girls from the school who were walking in the same direction, swinging their school bags, joking, humming snatches of popular tunes, making plans for the weekend.

'Bye Amy – see you,' they shouted as she turned into a baker's shop – but she wondered if she would see them again.

Once more, Dad had been surprisingly right about the weather. It had started to rain heavily blowing about in flurries of wind so there seemed to be no escape from getting soaked. People were hurrying off the streets and cars made a "whooshing" noise as they were driven quickly along the roads, splashing anyone who came too near.

Instead of waiting in a doorway for a few minutes,

Alice decided to rush along in the hope that Thomas would be early, then she could get back home quickly with the money and everything would be alright – she didn't like to think what would happen if it had all been lost, and knew that dabbling in stocks and shares was a risk.

She hated the road leading down to the canal with its blank, dark houses and mean alleyways, and her little room at Rosetti Grove suddenly seemed the safest and best place to be in the world. After all this was sorted out, she'd wish herself back to her real home again.

Christmas would be here soon, her grandfather would be up from the country to see them and take her and Lucy to a show in town. She wanted to chat to Lucy again and see Bunny and Terry and Alabaster, even at the cost of Huxley House and Zelda and Connie.

She had come to the track beside the canal, rough with waves this evening. The large black bulk of the disused warehouse on the left resembled a fortress, standing up to the fierce assaults of the weather.

*Please let Thomas be there,* she prayed, running over to the Penny Whistle and scrambling on to the small deck. She tried to slide back the door but it was locked and no one came to open it even though she hammered on it.

She would have to wait – it wouldn't be six o'clock for about another forty minutes. She was wet right through and shivering in the chill wind and she looked around for somewhere to shelter. The boat repairs shop was locked and a few derelict buildings nearby were open to the weather. Only the warehouse seemed to offer any hope of shelter.

The lower door was locked but seeing some steps going to the side nearby, she decided to see if there was another way in. The steps had been newly repaired by the builders and led up to a smaller door; it looked thick and unyielding but when Alice tried the latch, it opened quite easily – someone had forgotten to lock it. She went inside to total darkness but was relieved to be out of the rain and wind, and felt in her pocket for a small torch of Amy's which she'd popped in that morning.

She didn't want to waste the battery but it gave a small comforting light and she shone it around the vast lofty space.

A strong gust of wind caught the door and it slammed to with a great echoing noise, followed, as the sound died away, by another altogether different noise – this one was muffled and indistinct and was like a cry. Alice felt her skin prickle with fear. Was the old warehouse haunted? Perhaps it was the ghost of some old bargee who had met with a violent death in another century.

There were sounds of knocking and battering now and the thought came to Alice that maybe it was one of the builders, still working there, and that would explain the unlocked door. She was a little reassured until the cry came again – it was too high pitched – could it be an animal trapped somewhere? She couldn't make out where it was coming from. As far as she could see, the huge, cavernous space was empty. She felt tempted to rush out and brave the elements again. With shaking hands, she shone the torch around and noticed, further along on the right, a brick wall going up to the ceiling.

What was behind it? Curious and hardly daring to look, she crept forward and then started back with a fright as more banging noises began.

*Amy wouldn't hang back like this,* she tried to tell herself, *she'd be more assertive and discover what was going on.* She braced herself and went to look behind the wall. As she approached it, she realised that it was the outer wall of a lift shaft, but the lift was missing.

Down the hole, she could see what must be the top. There was a stout rope at each side but nothing was moving.

She called, with Amy's voice, 'Hello – anyone there?' The wind outside rattled the windows and she could hardly hear the muffled shout which came back. Somebody was imprisoned in the lift which had somehow stopped between the thick floors.

Shining her torch upwards, she could see the ropes going up to a pulley. She had seen something like it before on one of Terry's cultural outings to a historic country house. He had painstakingly explained to her the workings of the "dumb waiter" as he called it – used to bring up food from the kitchen and dining room, appearing like a small moveable cupboard and worked by pulling the ropes on adjusting weights.

This one would have been used to transport heavy goods up and down in the warehouse and was larger but worked on the same principle.

Alice could see that the heavy weight was attached to one of the ropes while the other one hung loosely, its ends frayed. She must find something to balance it which would bring the lift up again, but what?

By a door in the far corner, she could see a pile of workmen's tools: a ladder, some planks of wood and a large bucket. It was heavy and cumbersome but she managed to drag the bucket along to the sides of the lift and, catching hold of the end of the rope, pulled it towards her and tied it firmly to the bucket's handle.

The hammering down below started again. Who or what was she going to find if she did succeed in bringing up the lift? Perhaps it would be better to do nothing. But she imagined being trapped like that herself. *It would be like suffocating,* she thought, *entombed in total darkness.* It was bad enough when you seemed to get stuck for a second before the lift opened in a department store.

The bucket wasn't really heavy enough to do the trick on its own; she'd have to find something to fill it. There was nothing suitable inside; she opened the door, which swung in the wind again and rushed down the steps. It would be wonderful if Thomas had arrived but there was no sign of him. She searched around in the rain, hardly able to see in the dark and nearly stumbled over a heap of builders' rubble. *Bricks! They might do.* She struggled up the steps with as many as she could carry, making four journeys, then sank down by the lift shaft out of breath. Would the knot that she'd tied be strong enough and would the handle of the bucket take the strain? She put the bricks in carefully one by one.

Suddenly, but very, very slowly, the lift started to rise with great creakings and groanings. It seemed to be stopping again, so she added another brick and gradually she could begin to see the top part of the inside. Whoever it was in there was quiet now – perhaps frozen with the fear that too much movement or noise would stop it again or send it crashing down to the bottom of the shaft.

Alice picked up the torch from the floor and shone it down, hardly daring to look. Something caught her eye. It gleamed in the light from the torch and looked like a luminous moth. It seemed to be embedded in black curls. A figure was crouched low and trembling in a corner of the lift, head bent, it slowly came fully into view. Alice stared at it in amazement as it slowly looked up and she came face to face with Chrissie.

'What are you doing here?' She reached forward and pulled Chrissie clear of the lift but she didn't say anything. She didn't look surprised to see Alice, just miserable and clung to her tightly.

A loud crash made them both jump. The door had banged open again and someone stood like a great dark shadow in the feeble light from the torch. The two girls clutched one another in fear.

'There you are!' It was Thomas's voice. 'Is that Chrissie with you – I thought I said...' but Chrissie started crying then, great gulping, noisy sobs, trying at the same time to explain.

'I heard you and Thomas... Penny Whistle, only wanted to... wanted to... The B Fund all gone... wanted to know... Saw Amy... hid but floor went down.' She was too exhausted and shocked to go on. Clinging to Alice she shivered.

'You thought you'd spy, did you,' but Thomas didn't sound too angry. 'I'll make us some tea, then we'd better get home and explain things.' He picked up Alice's bag of shopping.

The interior of the Penny Whistle seemed snug now. The lamp was lit and a pot of tea made. Thomas found a couple of blankets. 'You both look a real mess – put these round you for a bit of warmth.' The two girls were covered in dust and debris. Alice had scratches and cuts and they were all soaking wet, but Thomas was grinning cheerfully.

'The money – the B Fund,' Alice said, 'what about the money?'

With a large smile, Thomas drew out of his pocket a wad of notes. 'It's all here and I've enough to pay off my debts and go back to college.' Chrissie listened as he explained briefly what had happened and about the information Alice had given him.

'I'm sorry Thomas – I didn't know you were in trouble,' she said. 'Sorry Amy.' She looked at Alice with large expressive eyes, which seemed to be apologising for a whole lot of other things apart from spying. Then she grinned slightly. 'You were great with that lift thing – I thought I was going to be stuck there for ever. Don't tell my Mum about it, she'd murder me.' Alice had to explain to Thomas about the lift, then all feeling a bit warmer, Thomas locked up the barge and they all walked back to Disraeli Drive, huddled under an oilskin cape they'd found, joking, laughing and singing snatches of Uncle Edgar's tune while the few people on the street crossed to the other side to avoid them.

'Thomas, Thomas.' Jimmy, pleased to have his eldest brother home unexpectedly, kept up a monotonous chant and was reluctant to go to bed. Aldous and Danny wanted to show Thomas their aeroplane models and dragged at his hand and even Evalina, usually preoccupied with her own affairs, looked glad to see him and gave him an account of her new job.

Only Dad looked solemn and he and Thomas had a talk privately in the sitting room, after which Thomas didn't look quite so much like a returning hero.

Chrissie had stayed on and helped Alice with the supper after they'd dried off, chatting and friendly now instead of scowling and sullen. She was giving a funny impersonation of a singer when her mother came through the back door and into the kitchen. 'I thought I'd find you here.' And she settled herself into a chair and looked as if she intended to stay for the night. Dad explained to her about Thomas in a few short words and she seemed a bit disappointed that things had been smoothed over so quickly – she liked a bit of drama and atmosphere. She managed a sorrowful shake of her head and a mournful, 'I don't know what the young are coming to.' She would obviously liked to have said 'What did I tell you,' but she hadn't guessed that the missing money would have had any connection with Thomas.

Now they were able to discuss plans again for the loft extension and work out a budget. Much later, Thomas yawned and said as Edgar was away, he'd go and sleep in the caravan and leave early for college the next morning. Jimmy had fallen asleep in an armchair and Aunt Seely was nodding over her coffee when the back door burst open.

'Hi folks, remember me?' Uncle Edgar, looking jaunty in a red cap, put his head round the door of the living room. He was smiling broadly 'Great news – listen to this,' and he launched into an account of his past few days which had included appearances at two clubs, the Tooty Fruity and the Green Cat, playing with his group.

'We gave them "Streetwise" – really gave it all we'd got and guess what? There, mingling with the crowd at the Green Cat was this talent scout, who said he liked it. "We might like to sign you to our label," he says, "a couple of CDs and possibly an album".' He paused for breath and gazed round with shining eyes. 'We've hit the jackpot! You'll be able to have a holiday in Barbados.'

'Hey steady on – don't get carried away,' Dad laughed. 'I'm really pleased but you're not just…'

Aunt Seely blinked and looked disapproving. 'Just talking big,' she muttered.

'Big talk, big buys –'

'He's only a fool… but streetwise,' Uncle Edgar quoted from his own song and glanced at Alice. *So he'd managed to finish the lyric,* she thought.

'But I'm not just being a fool – we *have* been signed up – all down in black and white.'

'Will you be famous?' Danny and Aldous were excited, 'and be on telly?'

'Who knows, who knows?'

Aunt Seely looked at Chrissie. 'You haven't done your homework yet, have you.' She stared round balefully at everyone else. 'I don't know what your poor mother is going to say about all this…'

Chrissie took Alice's arm as they went out. 'Don't forget, skating Sunday evening – I'll call for you.'

It seemed like a question so Alice said, 'Thanks, I'm

looking forward to it,' and hoped Amy would enjoy her evening. She wanted to escape upstairs to the bedroom where she could concentrate on wishing herself back to being Alice Fraser. She shouted 'Goodnight!' to everyone, sad at the thought of leaving them. At the bottom of the stairs, Thomas caught up with her. 'I won't forget how you helped me – I'll always remember it. You're such a good kid, stay exactly as you are, Amy – don't ever change.'

Alice smiled to herself – she was going to change, any minute now and she ran up the stairs away from the evenings' explosion of noise and excitement.

She closed the bedroom door and sat on the bed. Closing her eyes, she tried to think herself back at Rosetti Grove. *I wish to be Alice Fraser – Alice Fraser back in my own home.*

There was none of the floating sensation she'd experienced before. Nothing seemed to have changed when she opened her eyes. Something had gone wrong – she was still Amy Formica. She was seized by the terrible fear that she was locked in someone else's life for ever and would never be able to be herself again. She wanted to scream and shout and jump out of her skin in panic, but she seemed to hear Bunny's calm voice, 'Whenever chaos threatens, I sit down, breath deeply and write a list.'

Alice took some deep breaths and tried to gather her facts together and make a list in her head, going over the events which led up to the identity change.

1.  I was at the zoo

2. I was in the Tropical House
3. I saw Amy with her family
4. I spied her through the leaves of that strange plant with the smell of peppermint.
5. I had stopped to sniff the petals and had wished.

The wish had been made at the same time as she had bent over a flower... an orchid, she remembered. There would be no chance of finding it again tonight but tomorrow she would have to get to the zoo.

# TEN

*Alice mustn't be forced to leave her school because of me,* Amy thought. She had tried hard during the next couple of days to be seen and not heard, but it wasn't easy for her – she liked to say what she thought and her defence of a girl called Liz, who was getting the worst of Monsieur Tati's sarcastic tongue, brought her another order mark.

The work was no problem now she had peace and quiet to study but she was afraid that Terry and Bunny were still considering another school, which would surely upset Alice.

Zelda had kept well away from her, except to shove a small parcel at her on Wednesday morning. 'Here you are,' she said, 'and you've promised not to say anything, haven't you?' It was the diary and that night, Amy put it back with the others in the small cupboard by the bed.

As the week progressed, Bunny and Terry became even more absorbed in their work for the Harrington Retail Park and the circulation problem. They discussed it over their breakfast, Terry even producing a dark crayon and drawing an alternative idea on the white table top, and although they tried to keep to their normal schedule and spend half an hour in the evening discussing current affairs with Amy, their minds were on other things and they were obviously eager to get back to the studio.

'I don't mind reading the papers on my own, honestly,' Amy told them. 'You go back to your work and when you've finished it, we can talk then.'

The idea of changing the routine had never occurred to them. 'Are you sure?' Bunny said with surprise. 'Well, I suppose we might. You see the big presentation of our design is on Monday and we must get it right by then. You go and practice your flute after you've read the *Reminder*. That will fill up the rest of the time quickly.'

'No,' said Amy, 'I think I'll go and play with Alabaster and then I might make some fudge if there's any sugar in the house.'

'You'll have to ask Connie about that,' Bunny said uncertainly.

Amy was sure she knew what Connie's answer would be. She hadn't been in the kitchen on her own since she had discovered that "the rations" had vanished. Connie seemed to be always there, watching over the room with hawk-like vigilance.

On Friday afternoon in the middle of a singing lesson, Amy was summoned to Mrs Winterbourne's office. Everyone stared at her with interest – you never knew what to expect if you were sent for by Mrs Winterbourne.

'Come along in and close the door.' The Head was seated behind a large mahogany desk in front of which was a small chair. Amy sat down and looked around while Mrs Winterbourne went on reading a pamphlet. The room was austere and smelt of furniture polish. A large portrait of a stern-faced elderly woman in a flowing black dress seemed to be gazing down on the proceedings.

Picking up a piece of paper, Mrs Winterbourne looked at Amy over her reading spectacles. 'Would you like to explain *this*?' she said in an icy voice. It was the petition. Amy had forgotten all about it.

'I see your name is at the top – I presume the whole idea is yours.'

'Well, it was just...' Amy began but Mrs Winterbourne ignored her.

'Do you realise what damage you do to our ideals at Huxley House with your ridiculous suggestion? You strike a blow at the very foundation of our principles. The uniform is a symbol of conformity, everyone a member of a corporate group. No one stepping out of line with eccentricity of dress or bizarre hair apparel!' She paused a second for breath.

'It's just that I thought the uniform needed cheering up a little.' Amy fingered her shirt. 'It's so drab and colourless – it really looks dowdy, you must agree.' She glanced up at Mrs Winterbourne, who had taken a sharp intake of breath.

'You dare to criticise the colour! Do you realise that this uniform,' her voice sank a little with emotion, 'was chosen fifty years ago by my mother!' She was speechless for a moment, moved by the remembrance.

Fifty years ago. That seemed a very long time to Amy – surely it would be a good idea for it to be redesigned and updated. She started to say so but Mrs Winterbourne cut her short.

'That's quite enough!' She drew herself up impressively. 'From being a quiet, unobtrusive member of our community you seem to have become disruptive and thoroughly self-confident to the point of challenging authority.' She picked up an envelope and took out a letter. 'I have written to your parents.' She added something at the end of the note and sealed the envelope. 'Give it to them this evening, please.'

Amy got up to go as Mrs Winterbourne symbolically tore the petition into shreds and put the pieces in the waste paper basket.

'It was only a hair band...' but the Head, with a pained expression on her face, was reaching for a sheaf of papers.

It didn't seem as if she had done anything to help the position at school – quite the reverse, things seemed to be going from bad to worse.

She arrived back at Rosetti Grove at tea time and as she said 'Goodbye' to Jinty and Harriet, she saw Connie's brother leaving the house. In the gathering dusk, she could see that he was carrying what looked like a fruit pie, balancing it carefully on one hand, while over his other arm was slung a white carrier bag. She stood and watched him saunter down the street until he turned the corner, then she ran up the steps of number eleven.

Bunny and Terry were on their way to have a consultation with a colleague.

'That was Connie's brother who just left wasn't it – he was carrying a pie and I'm sure...' But they were disinterested in Amy's information.

'I expect so – now, we'll be back for Q.H. and don't forget the Prescotts are coming with their friends from television.

Amy remembered the letter she had to deliver. 'Mrs Winterbourne sent this.'

'What is it – another appeals letter?' Terry put down the roll of papers he was carrying and torn open the envelope. Bunny peered over his shoulder.

'Flouting authority... Inciting others to rebellious behaviour... What's all this about, Alice?'

'It's just about an old hair band, that's all.'

Terry looked perplexed. 'A hair band?'

'Well, art orientated or not, this school is obviously not suiting Alice – we'll have to think again. We're going to be late.' Bunny looked at her watch. As they went out, Amy heard her say something about 'Parkwood High.'

So it looked as if Alice was going to have to change schools after all and it was all her fault. She felt guilty. Sam had said he went to Parkwood High, she hoped Alice wouldn't mind the move too much.

A faint but wonderful smell of sizzling sausages seemed to be coming from the kitchen. Amy followed her nose hopefully but there was just the usual thin cut bread and butter with, today, the addition of a shortbread biscuit. The kitchen window was open, although it was very cold outside, and Connie was busy wiping the already immaculate work tops. 'I have to go out shortly for a while. You'll be alright,' it was more a statement than a question.

When Connie had gone, Amy had a quick look round the kitchen to see if any more "rations" had been hidden away but, of course, there were none now.

Everything was white and sterile, even the smell of sausages had gone. Amy closed the windows and went out to feed Alabaster.

'Hi, I'm coming to see your rabbit today, remember?' Sam was already climbing over the wall. It was freezing in the outhouse and the light from the single hanging bulb was poor.

'Let's take him in to the house,' Sam suggested.

Amy carried Alabaster carefully into the kitchen, while Sam looked around. 'I've never seen anywhere so... clean – is all your house like this?'

'Yes, all of it.'

'I don't believe it... you must have *one* room that's a mess.'

'No – come and see,' and Amy, still carrying the struggling rabbit, led the way upstairs.

In the sitting room, Sam stared round at the spotless serenity. 'You should see our house – chaos and confusion. It'll be weeks before we begin to get straight. Books everywhere, we can't find a thing.' Amy thought it sounded more homely than number eleven and more like six Disraeli Drive; she felt a sudden pang as she thought of home.

'What's that?' Sam, with his head turned sideways, was looking at the new painting.

'It's called "Repression" and I think it's meant to say things to you.'

'Well, it must be speaking in double Dutch; I can't understand it.'

Alabaster, becoming bored, suddenly made a bid for freedom; he lunged with scrabbling claws out of Amy's arms and loped across the room with surprising speed.

'Quick, catch him – he'll make an awful mess!' Amy shouted and she and Sam darted over the grey carpet between the angular grey chairs, knocking over Terry's twisted metal standard lamp, which in turn brought "Repression" crashing down from its precarious picture hook.

Pausing for a second to allow Sam to draw near, the rabbit then scampered behind the beige curtains, coming out again the other side and shattering an artistic arrangement of white twigs.

It had become a game now. Half laughing and half shrieking, Amy and Sam gave chase, but Alabaster was adept at dodging and seemed to be enjoying his new found freedom. Amy could understand it, she too felt as if she had been cooped up too long and was glad to let off steam.

Too late they saw the sitting room door was open and Alabaster hopped speedily towards it and bounded up the stairs. Reaching the studio before Amy, he disappeared behind a plans chest.

The white calm of the room was shattered while Sam waved rolls of paper up and down to encourage the rabbit to jump out and Amy moved a drawing board to block the other side.

Suddenly, looking like a giant animated powder puff, Alabaster sprang.

Amy screamed and lunged forward to grab him while Sam yelled: 'Get him!'

He was heavy and wouldn't stop wriggling. Amy tottered, Sam tried to help but they ended up in a heap bumping into a table and scattering a model which lay on a base board, on which had been composed a number of carefully placed blocks of different sizes.

Amy was still clutching the furiously scrabbling animal. She and Sam rushed quickly downstairs with him and put him back safely in his hutch, breathing a sigh of relief.

It was strange to see the sitting room in such disarray. 'We'd better do something about this mess – it's beginning to look like our house!' Sam said and started to pick up a few of the twigs, jabbing them unceremoniously back into their jar. Amy went to inspect the standard lamp, wondering if it had always had that particular dent at the top.

Sam knocked the picture hook into the wall more firmly with his shoe and rehung "Repression" and then together they tried to remove evidence of white rabbit fur from the dark carpet.

'I think that'll do, let's have a look upstairs,' and Amy led the way up to the studio.

While Sam moved back the drawing board and straightened the pile of rolled plans, Amy went to see what it was they'd knocked flying.

'Oh no – look at this – it's their model – the very important one they're working on!' In one corner of the board was the name "Harrington Retail Park". Transparent tape ran in different directions looking as if it marked out the roads; little square pieces of plastic with "C.P." written on them probably represented car parks, but the blocks showing the buildings had shifted, some on to the floor and they didn't know how to begin to rearrange them.

'What on earth can we do?' Amy was shocked.

'A crisis,' Sam agreed.

'Mmm – big trouble.' They looked at the board despairingly and then listened nervously as they heard the muffled *bang* of the front door down below, then soft footsteps coming up the stairs.

'It's Connie coming back.' Amy whispered. 'She's going to her room – you'd better go.' Quickly and haphazardly they placed the small balsa wood blocks back on the model, then crept downstairs to the kitchen.

'Hope it's alright about the model.' Sam opened the back door, went into the garden and started to climb over the wall. 'We usually have spaghetti for lunch on Sunday – I'll tell Mum to ring your mother so you can come.' He had jumped down the other side and Amy just caught these words as they became more faint.

'Thanks!' she shouted back. *Alice might be glad of a new friend,* she thought, though he might not be allowed inside number eleven, if it was discovered that she and Sam had wrecked the Retail Park.

Bunny and Terry were late getting back. By the time they had quickly "spruced up" as Terry called it, it was half past seven. The time for Quality Hour had evaporated altogether and someone was ringing the front doorbell. Bunny frantically consulted her watch. 'It must be the Prescotts already. I am sorry about this,' she said to Amy, 'we'll make up the extra time over the weekend I promise. We'll experiment with some gouaches.'

'It's alright, honestly – you don't have to organise things all the time…' Amy started to say, then stopped, realising that she was speaking for Alice, who perhaps enjoyed an ordered, predictable regime.

Bunny gave a tired smile, 'Perhaps you're right – I do…' but the bell rang loud and shrill once more and she broke off her sentence to go and open the door.

*Thank goodness they hadn't noticed anything different about the sitting room,* Amy thought with relief, *and hadn't had time yet to go up to the studio – a short reprieve before the storm.*

The clear penetrating tones of the Prescotts could be heard in the hall and on the stairs.

'Julia and Charles Rennie – they've been longing to meet you – Charles is producing a rather outré programme next month. It's called *Winter Altruism*, isn't it? You must tell us all about it!' The voices came nearer and then suddenly the room seemed to be filled with people: Amanda Prescott, lean and elegant, like her husband, James, and the Rennies – Charles short and comfortable looking and Julia who looked kindly and studious.

Bunny and Terry fussed around with mineral water and fruit juices and Amy passed round a plate of dry biscuits which looked like cardboard. The talk was of a book Charles had written and a lecture on Beethoven which Julia was to deliver shortly. Amanda looked down her nose at Amy and took one of the biscuits. 'This one's quite musical, aren't you Alice?' she said loudly. 'The flute, loves performing too – what's it to be this evening, Mozart again?' and she smiled a condescending smile at Amy.

'That would be lovely,' Julia Rennie said, 'if you don't really mind – I used to hate it when I was your age.'

'Yes, go and fetch your flute, Alice,' Terry said. 'She's been learning a piece called "Firefly".' Everyone looked expectantly at Amy, who stood quite still, not knowing what to say.

'Go on Alice – go and bring your flute down.' Bunny was looking a little impatient.

'I expect she likes lots of pleading and coaxing,' Amanda Prescott said with a shrug. 'Well, I'm afraid I don't have time for that sort of tendency.'

How could she save Alice's face, Amy wondered – what could be substituted for the performance of "Firefly" – she played no musical instruments herself and had never even discovered the whereabouts of the flute.

The Rennies were still looking expectant, Bunny and Terry disappointed and Amanda had turned away to say something to her husband.

In as loud a voice as she could muster, Amy said, 'I'm sorry, I left my flute at school, but I can sing if you'd like.'

A murmur of interest went round as she went to stand by the window.

'It's called "Streetwise",' she announced. It was Uncle Edgar's song with a haunting tune and catchy rhythm, and she enjoyed singing it, keeping the beat by swaying, tapping her feet and clapping her hands over her head. The fourth verse was still unfinished so she sang the first three over again.

'He's still sure he's very cool and streetwise,' she finished.

There was silence for a minute, which was pierced by Amanda Prescott's shrill laugh. 'A jingle for an advert I expect.' Her words sounded like a sneer.

Amy saw that Bunny and Terry looked astonished by her performance but Charles Rennie's face broke into a big smile. 'Encore!' he shouted. 'That was terrific – marvellous beat!' and Julia clapped her hands, 'It certainly has something!'

'I'll sing it again and perhaps you'd all like to snap your fingers to the beat,' Amy said relaxing. While the others snapped and clapped enthusiastically, Amanda turned to study "Repression" and at the finish of the song launched into an account of the exhibition where she had spotted the painting and advised Bunny and Terry to purchase it.

'Yes, I'm afraid I'm to blame,' she said, as if playfully scolding herself, 'but to me it epitomises the battle for the soul of modernisation.'

Amy saw Julia Rennie's eyebrow go up and Charles inclined his head a little as if trying to comprehend both the painting and Amanda's statement.

Bunny and Terry were busy refilling glasses.

'Yes,' Amanda continued, 'it has this progressive quality – in aesthetic terms – of rising above its time... the placement of that arc and the sweep of that curve – just perfect. In fact it's so moving that... I could weep. Yes, I could.' Everyone seemed impressed by the sensitivity of her feelings except Amy, who thought *Yuck!*

Terry, handing an orange juice to Charles Rennie, glanced up at the picture and frowned slightly.

'Hang on a minute. It's upside down!'

Bunny, before she could stop herself, let out a yell of laughter and so did Amy. Charles and Julia turned away quickly but Amy could see Charles was biting his lip and Julia was smiling.

James Prescott swiftly took out his handkerchief and blew his nose loudly, while his wife flushed a dull red, put down her glass, looked at her watch and said, 'Is that the time – we must be off – dining with the Ledgers.' Amy noticed that Terry's shoulders were shaking up and down as he adjusted "Repression" and as soon as Amanda had swept out with as much dignity as she could muster, followed by James and Bunny, he laughed so much that tears came to his eyes and Charles and Julia joined in.

Conversation was more relaxed after that and Amy enjoyed hearing about the Rennie's dog, Mac. After they had gone, Bunny lounged back as far as she was able in one of the uncomfortable grey chairs, 'We haven't had any supper yet – I just don't know where the time has gone – we're really off schedule.'

'I'll make some sandwiches, and we can eat here in front of the fire,' said Amy.

'Then we'll have to get back to the drawing board.' Terry sighed. 'I'd like some ham and pickle sandwiches or sardine and tomato.'

'I don't think we've got any of those things – there is hardly any food in the house, I've been trying to tell you,' Amy said.

'No food in the house?' Now that she felt very hungry, Bunny was suddenly interested in the topic. 'We give Connie plenty of housekeeping money – what on earth does she spend it on?'

Amy shrugged and went downstairs to see what she could find. The front doorbell rang as she reached the hall.

Opening the door, she saw a plump middle-aged man muffled up in tweed coat and woolly scarf. He looked serious. 'Mr Cooper of "Coopers",' he announced himself. 'It's no good ringing is it – get nowhere – your parents in?'

Amy called up to Bunny and Terry and then went into the kitchen but she couldn't concentrate on sandwiches as sounds of an argument came from the hall.

'I can't understand it,' she heard Bunny say, then a second later Terry sounded puzzled, 'I certainly haven't eaten chicken breasts or asparagus tips, let alone packets of smoked salmon – the freezer part of our fridge is always empty!'

Mr Cooper's gruff voice interrupted, 'No payment for weeks – credit is credit but…'

Amy crept forward into the hall. 'I think that stock of food I saw in the oven is something to do with it – it vanished. Connie called them "emergency rations"…'

'Yes, I do remember you saying something about food in the oven. Connie!' Terry shouted up the stairs.

Connie came down slowly and sullenly. At first, when confronted with the bills, she denied all knowledge of the expenditures and provisions, but then she sat down heavily on one of the stair treads. She tried to explain how her brother, much younger than she was, had always been spoilt and pampered and used to the luxuries of life, never in any permanent work but frittering away any money that came his way on gambling.

'He always managed to get round me,' Connie whined, 'it's all his fault.' She had juggled the accounts, paying a little here and a little there as she owed money at various shops, always managing to keep just a little ahead of herself, hoarding tins and heaping little gifts on the brother. Now, bitterly, she piled the blame on him.

'Well, I hope he looks after you now as well as you've looked after him,' Terry said quietly.

She understood, thankfully, that he wasn't going to prosecute and went silently back up to her room to pack, while Bunny wrote out a cheque for Mr Cooper.

They had jam sandwiches standing up in the kitchen, while promising themselves a shopping spree for food the next day.

'You know, I think we can manage without a "Connie" now,' Terry said. 'Alice is becoming quite practical and I used to enjoy cooking when I was a student. 'Toad in the hole,' he reminisced, 'and syrup pudding.'

Bunny looked doubtful but brightened when Amy suggested she could organise a brand new schedule.

'Now – back to work,' Terry groaned, 'and see if the puzzle can be solved. We'll be burning the midnight oil tonight.'

Oh no! Amy heard them go up to the studio and counted to three for the howl of rage that would come when they saw their ruined model, the shambles that now represented the Harrington Retail Park.

There was nothing to be heard for a few moments, she imagined their silent horror, then she clutched the banister rail and closed her eyes as she heard a yell.

But it didn't sound quite the cry of horror she'd expected – it was different, it sounded... jubilant.

'Eureka!'

Amy ran up the stairs two at a time.

Their faces looking pleased and excited, Bunny and Terry were pouring over the model.

'Problem solved! It all works – it's all come right! How did that happen?'

Amy gave a little cough and Terry turned round.

'Do you know anything about this?'

'Well, it was Alabaster really – he was running round and it got joggled and Sam and I...'

Terry shook his head in bewilderment. 'Alabaster? And who's Sam? Never mind, go on.'

'I tried to put the blocks back but we couldn't remember where they'd gone. Sam did most of them – he lives next door and goes to Parkwood High.'

'A boy of some perception.' Terry went back to studying the Retail Park and Bunny nodded in agreement.

Amy left them and went to her bedroom. Things hadn't worked out too badly. The silence of the house engulfed her. She thought of her room at home – what would they all be doing at this moment? She missed her noisy, boisterous family: Danny, Aldous, Jimmy even Evalina with her grumbling and Chrissie with her uncertain moods. She missed Uncle Edgar's music and most of all Dad and Mum, who would be home soon.

Well, so would she be home soon to welcome her. She'd go right now – this very minute, and Alice could step back into her own shoes.

She screwed up her eyes to concentrate and thought about her family.

*I wish… to be myself again, to be Amy Formica,* and she waited for the strange feeling of being drawn down to the centre of the earth to come again, the feeling she had experienced with the other wish, but nothing happened. Opening her eyes, with growing fear, she looked in the mirror. Nothing had changed – she was still Alice Fraser.

# ELEVEN

She was still Alice Fraser! Amy kept looking at her reflection in the mirror – how could she ever get back to being herself. She couldn't stand the idea of being trapped in someone else's body and not be recognised again by her own family. How had she swapped places? Was there more to it than just wishing? She thought back to last Sunday, it seemed years ago.

*I was standing in the Tropical House and saw Alice standing on her own, looking quiet and peaceful. There was a huge orchid – the Rainbow Orchid – I looked through the leaves and smelt one of the flowers and at the same time I wished I could be her – I didn't mean for ever. Perhaps if I go to exactly the same spot and do everything the same as I did last time... I must go to the zoo tomorrow.*

Terry was feeling relaxed and cheerful, the circulation problems of the Retail Park having been solved and he and Bunny were looking forward to a morning's shopping at a large supermarket. 'We'll all go together, it'll be quite a novelty and we'll stock up our shelves and refrigerator. I want to make a chilli con carne,' he announced at breakfast on Saturday morning. 'And on Saturday afternoon...'

Amy held her breath – she just wanted to go to the zoo and as quickly as possible. '... what would you like to do – you choose, anything you like – within reason. If it hadn't been for you and your friend, we'd still have our noses to the grindstone today and probably all of Sunday too!'

'I'd love to go to the zoo again,' Amy said quickly, 'I want to do some sketching in the Tropical House. There's a plant there with unusual colours.'

Terry looked up approvingly. 'Right, the zoo it is. Perhaps I'll bring my sketching pad along as well. How would that be? And I've had another idea – perhaps Sam would like to come too!'

Amy had hoped to go off on her own into the Tropical House. Now it looked as if she'd have to shake off Sam as well as Terry, but she said, 'Yes, that'd be great.' Alice might be glad to have a friend next door. Bunny's usual Saturday timetable seemed to have been abandoned and without Connie hovering around in her white overall, breakfast stretched into late morning. Terry had even unearthed a packet of oats from the back of a cupboard and had made a huge bubbling pan of porridge.

\*\*\*

Thomas had left early to get back to college again in time

for exams and the next excitement would be Mum's homecoming party the following day, Sunday. Aldous and Danny were already making a large "WELCOME HOME MUM" sign, helped by Jimmy. Uncle Edgar joined them for a late breakfast but did more talking than eating, still elated by his success and the opening of new opportunities.

'This girl here,' he pointed at Alice, 'helped me get my song together – that last little bit … it made all the difference,' he said generously, taking a small bite from a piece of toast. 'Now what can I do for you? You name it – something special to show my appreciation.'

'I'd like to go to the zoo,' Alice said, jumping at the chance without any hesitation.

Uncle Edgar choked on a crumb; he'd been expecting something more tangible, like a camera or…

'If that's what you want, you shall have your wish. We'll go this afternoon and have tea there!'

'We went last Sunday on my birthday,' Danny said, looking up.

'And I want to go again,' Alice said firmly.

'I want to come,' Jimmy shouted. Maybe it would be a help to have Jimmy there too, Alice thought – Uncle Edgar could take him to see the penguins being fed while she vanished to the Tropical House.

'Short periods of sun today – temperatures warmer than average,' Dad had predicted. He was going to see a builder friend of Edgar's that afternoon to discuss the transformation of the loft. *I still haven't found out what Dad's job is, now I'll never know*, Alice reflected.

He was right about the weather – the sun shone

through a November mist as she, with Uncle Edgar and Jimmy, set off for the zoo. She looked back at Aldous and Danny who were outside struggling with their "Welcome Home" banner, wondering how to fix it over the front door. Evalina had her head out of the bedroom window and was giving directions in a loud and bossy manner. Half of her felt miserable to be leaving them as she waved and they all yelled 'Goodbye!' She held Jimmy's hand tightly.

It was pleasant wandering round in the pale afternoon sunlight, looking at the animals. They passed the tea shop, where she remembered leaving Connie and her heart sank at the thought of her.

Now they were coming to the Tropical House. Her heart beating furiously, she steeled herself to say casually, 'I just want to look at a plant in there which we're doing in Biology – won't be a minute – why don't you two go and get an ice cream?' She knew this idea would be popular with Jimmy.

'Sounds like a good idea, c'mon young James.' Jimmy clung to Alice's hand for a moment, then Uncle Edgar swung him up onto his shoulders. Alice watched them go, then turned away with tears in her eyes; it was more painful than she would have believed, parting from them and she wasn't even able to say goodbye properly.

The Tropical House was overpoweringly hot with the addition of the sun pouring through the glass. Alice worked her way quickly through ferns and palms, looking urgently for the orchid in amongst the dense foliage.

The visit to the supermarket had been a success. Bunny and Amy had enjoyed composing a long and comprehensive list of all essentials, and a few non essentials, for the food cupboard and they had all concocted a delicious lunch. After the syrup pudding, Terry looked as if he was going to fall asleep in one of his grey, uncomfortable chairs; he even suggested some feather cushions might be a good idea and didn't disagree when Amy suggested they might be pale green. His eyelids drooped and Amy felt worried. She was eager to get to the Tropical House and find the orchid.

'Don't forget we're going to the zoo,' she reminded him and he made an effort to rouse himself. They collected Sam, who invited Amy back to supper at his house. Bunny was enjoying a browse through a book called *Farmhouse Cooking* subtitled *those true authentic country flavours our grandparents knew,* which someone had given them as a Christmas present years ago and had never been opened.

'Are you off?' she looked up at Amy and smiled, 'I think we'll have "Cottage Kitchen Pie" for lunch tomorrow – it sounds very tasty.'

Amy nearly said, 'I hope it turns out alright,' but stopped herself. She gave Bunny a quick kiss goodbye – she felt sad and must have looked sad as Bunny said, 'You're only going to the zoo!'

It felt almost like being on holiday as she and Sam ran from enclosure to paddock watching Terry do quick sketches of animals and people.

'Can we go to the Aquarium?' Sam asked. 'We're going to have a fish tank at home with sea horses and angel fish and some of those tiny luminous ones!'

'I've been thinking of getting one of those too. Very relaxing after a day's work to watch them swimming round and round, through the rocks and coral.' Terry waved his hands eloquently. 'And you can get sunken galleons to put at the bottom of the tank, and mermaids…'

The two were hardly aware of Amy, who interrupted them. 'I just want to finish a sketch I was making last week in the Tropical House. I'll catch you up.' They nodded briefly and Amy saw them go, talking animatedly into the entrance to the Aquarium. Then they were gone.

Not giving herself time for regrets, Amy hurried into the steamy heat of the Tropical House. The jungle-like luxuriant vegetation seemed to drip from everywhere. Trying to remember where she had seen the orchid, she darted between exotic blossoms and lush creepers. It was like a maze and somewhere near the centre would be the plant she was looking for.

*I'm sure it was just about here.* Yes, there was the display of orchids again but in the middle where the special one should have been, there was a space. The notice in front still read "Rainbow Orchid from the Crystall Islands, believed to have magical properties", but there was no sign of it.

Frantically, Amy pushed aside the leaves of surrounding plants and searched around. The tendrils of an overhanging vine seemed to reach out to entwine her and she felt engulfed in greenery. Parting the foliage, she peered through, then cried out with shock. Gazing at her from the other side was the image she had seen in her mirror for so many years – she had come face to face with herself.

Her other self looked stunned with amazement. Both reached out to touch the other, to reassure themselves that they weren't seeing their reflections in a looking glass.

'You're me!'

'I'm you, aren't I?'

'I want to change back.'

'I want to be myself again.'

They spoke urgently at the same time.

'It's something to do with the Rainbow Orchid, isn't it?'

'Where is it?'

'It's gone!'

Both felt frozen with shock and fear, realising they might never be recognised as their real selves again. What could they do now? They felt powerless.

'What's all the noise?'

A uniformed attendant had materialised from behind a potted palm. The Tropical House was usually a place of sultry calm, quiet except for a babbling from a small indoor waterfall.

Amy thought quickly. 'We're really interested in these orchids – we're doing a project on them at school. We specially wanted to see the Rainbow Orchid but it doesn't seem to be here.'

'Well, it's nice to see you taking an interest. I've a

little greenhouse at home and grow one or two specimens myself.'

Alice hopped from leg to leg hardly able to contain her impatience.

'We had to move the Rainbow a couple of days ago – she was looking a bit droopy.' He paused sorrowfully as if talking of an old friend, while the two girls looked horror struck. 'But cheer up,' he was surprised to see their appalled expressions, 'it's not that bad. We've put her in the little glass house round at the side,' he pointed vaguely to the right, 'and she's coming along nicely, thanks to a ...'

But they didn't wait to hear the rest, they were rushing in the direction he had pointed.

There, inside the small greenhouse, standing in all its glory, was the Rainbow Orchid; pale, soft petals of subtle colours which seemed to reach out inviting you to smell their scent.

Alice shouted with relief. 'Quickly, let's wish!'
But Amy said, 'I think we have to smell the flower and wish at the same time. That's what I did before.' Alice did remember the surprising scent of peppermint which she had sniffed.

They each chose a bloom and with desperate concentration, they closed their eyes and wished with all their might. Alice felt herself floating up, up as the familiar scent overpowered her and seemed to overwhelm her. Her thoughts became fragmented, like tiny pieces of mosaic, getting smaller and smaller. Aunt Seely, Chrissie's hair slide, Jimmy's bright blue sweater. Evalina's wig, the kitchen curtains at Disraeli Drive. They were all receding. She opened her eyes.

As Amy breathed in deeply, she was being drawn down, pulled by an invisible magnet into a decreasing spiral. As she went down, ribbons of film danced before her mind's eye clearly and then started fading away; a film of neutral shades showing Amanda Prescott laughing, Connie hiding a fruit cake, Bunny flitting like a delicate moth, holding a white rabbit, flying further and further away. They were gone. She opened her eyes.

'Here Amy, ice cream.' It was Jimmy holding out a cornet to her and running a practiced tongue round his own chocolate wafer. Amy's face burst into a big smile. He knew her – she was herself again. She bent down and hugged him and the ice creams until he squealed indignantly. 'What're you doing?' he shouted.

Uncle Edgar joined them. 'Time we were getting back,' he looked at his watch, taking no notice of Alice, 'unless you want your tea here.'

'Home for tea,' Amy said firmly. She looked at Alice – there was so much they had to talk about and explain to each other but now there was no time. She took Jimmy's free hand and the three of them went towards the door. Amy hesitated and looked back at Alice, wanting to say something.

'Come on Amy,' Uncle Edgar shouted. Alice, for a moment, went instinctively to join them and then remembered. She felt forlorn suddenly.

Uncle Edgar started to whistle his tune and held open the door for the two people coming through; they smiled and thanked him looking past Amy and Jimmy to where Alice stood.

A shaft of pale sunlight caught Alice's eye, she could

just see a boy approaching, whom she'd never seen before. Then she heard a familiar voice.

'There you are, Alice, we've been searching for you – have you finished your sketch?' Shielding her eye she saw that it was Terry and with a great rush of relief, realised that he recognised her. She felt in the pocket of her old camel coloured coat for the sketchbook, yes – it was there. 'Not quite, but I think I'm ready to go home now,' and she smiled a smile nearly as big as Amy's.

'Hey, don't forget you're coming to have a meal with us,' the boy said and Terry laughed. 'Had you forgotten?'

They went out into the late afternoon sun. It was turning cold now and a hazy mist was rising. In the distance, Alice could just make out the figures of Uncle Edgar and Amy, each holding a hand of Jimmy and swinging him as they walked. For a brief second, Amy turned her head, looked back at Alice and smiled. Then they disappeared into the mist.

# EPILOGUE

It was not quite Christmas yet but for Alice, the joy of the festive season had arrived already. She had spent her last day at Huxley House – she and Lucy were to start next term at Parkwood High, already attended by her new friend Sam. She was still not sure how this had happened. Bunny and Terry had been quite decisive about it and Alice kept quiet, not wanting to risk her luck. Zelda had been no more trouble to her – in fact she'd kept out of her way, almost deliberately and somehow or other, her precious diary had found it's way back to her cupboard.

Added to all this, the hated Connie had vanished without trace; shopping and cooking had turned into an enjoyable chore shared by all and the fixed schedule previously ruling the life of the house had been relaxed into something Bunny now called "Flexitime", which meant time could be adapted to fit in with whatever they wanted to do. Life had changed for the better in so many ways that Alice could hardly believe it. Also, Amanda Prescott with her mocking laugh hadn't been seen for several weeks.

Now and then she thought of the family at Disraeli Drive, especially one Saturday morning when she and Terry were decorating the Christmas tree and she heard a familiar tune on the radio – it was turned down low but she could hear the unmistakeable beat of "Streetwise". Terry had heard it too and had started whistling as if he knew it as well.

***

Amy struggled into the sitting room with the large Christmas tree helped by Danny and Aldous. Aunt Seely had said it was far too big but everyone else loved its height and shape; it should look magnificent and glittering, a symbol of celebration.

There was a lot to celebrate this Christmas: Mum was home and doing well – sitting on the sofa with her feet up, reading to Jimmy and watching the tree being put up. Despite Aunt Seely's dire warnings, she would be able to return to her teaching in the New Year.

Thomas had somehow scraped through his exams and Uncle Edgar was making plans to go on tour with the Sugarbeats and bring out an album of his own compositions. His caravan vibrated with music and rhythm more these days and Dad said he looked forward to some peace and quiet when he'd gone.

Amy's mind flickered back to the silence of Rosetti Grove – she was looking forward to finding a sanctuary from the noise and clamour of family life up in the new room; work had already started on it and she had been given credit for the idea.

Chrissie had called round to help with the decorations, no longer sulky and sullen. She had shown no jealousy even when Amy, to her own surprise, had been given a part in the "Insect Play" to be put on next term.

*\*\**

Both trees sparkled with a glittering and bewitching brilliance. In Rosetti Grove, the living room was transformed by the splendour of the multi-coloured decorations hanging from the branches: blue, red, green, gold. There were yellow fairy lights and great big purple baubles, orange stars and a fairy, perched up on top of this glowing myriad of colour, with a bright pink wand. Alice smiled.

At six, Disraeli Drive, Amy put the finishing touches to her tree and stood back, pleased by the effect. The shape was lined with silver tinsel, silver frost and fairy lights twinkled; small silver baubles were suspended from the boughs: it looked beautiful. 'Perfect for ones visual concepts,' as Bunny might have said.